Fanny Wheeler Hart

Freda

A Novel: Vol. II.

Fanny Wheeler Hart

Freda
A Novel: Vol. II.

ISBN/EAN: 9783337065164

Printed in Europe, USA, Canada, Australia, Japan

Cover: Foto ©Andreas Hilbeck / pixelio.de

More available books at **www.hansebooks.com**

A Novel.

BY THE

AUTHOR OF "MRS. JERNINGHAM'S JOURNAL."

IN THREE VOLUMES
VOL. II.

LONDON:

RICHARD BENTLEY AND SON,

Publishers in Ordinary to Her Majesty the Queen.

1878.

CONTENTS OF VOL. II.

FREDA.

CHAPTER I.

HOW THEY WERE MARRIED.

MAJOR and Mrs. Cameron did not appear to have been at all alarmed at their niece's long and lonely absence, in the midst of a dreadful thunderstorm; nor did this appearance belie the reality. In fact, they were people who were *not* soon alarmed. Easy and good-natured, living solely for amusement and finding that amusement in very small trifles, they had led a comfortable life, and had allowed this life of comfort to be very little disturbed by having an unexpected niece thrown suddenly

on their hands. They had never been unkind
to her, they had wished her to be as comfortable as themselves, and they had taken no
trouble about her in any way whatever.

When she now came home to them wet
through, and introduced to them a wet
stranger, who was also one of the handsomest
young men they had ever seen, very little
impression was produced on them, and they
were neither excited nor interested. She
had gone out and she had come in, she had
been caught in the rain, and she had lost
her way. Somebody had, naturally enough,
turned up to help her, and she had brought
that somebody home with her, and as that
somebody was evidently quite a proper person
for them to associate with, and very much
inclined to associate with them, there was no
harm done, and everything was as pleasant
as everything ought always to be.

Lionel Fane soon received a *carte blanche*
to visit at the house as often and in as friendly
a manner as even he could desire. Her uncle
and aunt still considered Freda as a child,
and they never connected her and his visits
together as cause and effect, but they had

ascertained, as those things always are ascertained, that he was respectable, and they heard at the same time that he was rich; though they did not care about that, as they did not see how it concerned them. When, at the end of a week, he offered for Freda, they were very much astonished. Mrs. Cameron asked him how old she was; and on his saying he neither knew nor cared, she applied to her husband for the information. They set their heads together, went back into the past, calculated, and surprised themselves, and each other, by the discovery that Freda was seventeen.

Mr. Fane remarked that he did not care whether Freda was seventeen or seventy; she was Freda, and that was all that mattered to him.

Mrs. Cameron rejoined that she was a complete child, and had no mind at all. The idea of Freda, a married woman, and the mistress of a household, was too ridiculous.

But again, that exactly suited Mr. Fane. He declared that Freda was almost preternaturally clever, as far as natural cleverness went; and that, as to a mind, he had never wished to marry a woman with a mind; his desire was to form his wife's mind himself—in that lay the secret of real happiness. Such a creature as Freda—found so early in her sweet life, that her mind might be formed by the husband whose home she was to adorn and whose days she was to glorify—could any prospect of human happiness excel that?

In fact, Mr. Fane was in love.

It was now the Major's turn to speak, and he announced with reluctance that Freda had nothing—literally not a penny. They supported her, but they could not dower her—and her parents had left her nothing.

The idea of Freda requiring a dower! she was a dower in herself. Support her! what a delicious task, to support her! Imagination could hardly go beyond the joy of supporting Freda. And then he poured out an account of his own ample means, his success in his profession, and the private fortune that made that success only necessary to his ambition, till the Major and Mrs. Cameron were amazed, and felt they had no right to stand in Freda's light, and make difficulties that might deprive her of such a prosperous future.

Besides which, it would be a great convenience not to have to take her to Jamaica.

But here was a fresh occasion for demur—the Major and his wife must sail for Jamaica on that day three weeks, and it might prove a very long engagement if they all waited till the return of the regiment.

Waited till the return of the regiment! waited for Freda!

Then Mr. Fane explained himself more fully than he had done yet, and declared that he had no desire in the world, no motive for living, no objection to dying, except that of marrying Freda before Major and Mrs. Cameron left England for Jamaica.

In fifteen minutes from the moment in which he made this speech, it was settled among the three that the thing could, should, and would be done.

Of course there was a fourth person to consult, but none of the three principals apprehended any opposition there.

The Camerons were accustomed to dispose of their niece when they disposed of themselves, and both having always intended her to marry as soon as she grew up, the only difficulty they had encountered had been, the bringing themselves to believe that she had grown up already.

Lionel Fane was strong in the memory that she had bought his photograph before she had ever heard of his existence, and that when she opened her radiant eyes upon him in the cave, she had at once said, "Oh, you have come—I am glad—I *wanted* you."

That was enough for the maiden to feel. The rest must all be left to *him*, and he was more than equal to the occasion. He should develop both heart and mind. He should form them both — beautiful and delightful task, rendering life a fairy dream of joy and love—in the thought of which he revelled, without one momentary fear that he might be incompetent to the work he was undertaking.

When Mrs. Cameron spoke to Freda on the interesting subject, she found her hardly as amenable as might have been expected. In fact her aunt had had her misgivings, and therefore while she had let it pass, when Lionel had requested that he might be the person to broach the subject to her, she had secretly resolved to prepare her wayward niece a little beforehand.

She had excused this treachery, to her husband and to herself, by saying, " Freda is such a child. It would not be right to let Mr. Fane speak first; it is my duty to prepare her, both for her own sake and his. She really would not understand."

And it is to be supposed that she did not, for when Mrs. Cameron gently broke the great news to her, she snapped her finger and thumb in her aunt's face, and said, " Rubbish ! Like his impudence ! I'd rather not !"

And indeed she took a great deal of talking to, before she would listen to reason; *so* much that Mrs. Cameron began to despair, and the Major had to be called in, of whom she was much fonder than she was of her aunt, perhaps because, like all other men, he was, though her uncle, still her slave.

A great deal was explained to Freda as to the eligibility of the offer ; of what her circumstances would be if she did not marry ; of how Mr. Fane was everything that the most fastidious, the most romantic, or the most worldly girl could wish for in a husband ; and of how he was so much in love with her he would do anything and every-thing she desired now, always, and for ever.

But the argument that made most impression on the young lady was the one she had quoted to Letty—that she must marry some day or other, and that she could never have so good an opportunity of doing so as this. Even then, when all it would entail was unknown to her, she disliked the idea of matrimony extremely ; but still, if it must be done, it must, and the sooner it was got over perhaps the better. She remembered how she had hated the idea of tucking up her hair, only she had been told that it was a thing that must be done, as she was so tall. She had resisted it as much as she could, and only did it at last on the principle that she was going to act on now—as it must be done, it must. She remembered how uncomfortable her head had felt for a day or two with coils of hair round it, and combs and pins in it, and how her shoulders had missed the flowing locks.

"But really only for a day or two," philosophised Freda ; "after that I got quite comfortable, and I am not sure that I *should* be comfortable now if I tumbled my hair all down again and went about with it so. Very likely having a house of my own and a husband will be just the same, and if so I had better be a good girl, make up my mind to it, and get it over. It certainly will be pleasant to be rich, to be able to do just what I like always in everything, and to have somebody to wait on me and obey me as my husband will, so I won't make any more fuss, but just do as I am bid."

Mr. Fane had never contemplated the possibility of a refusal, but he was not the less in the seventh heaven of blissful rapture when he was accepted. Freda did not keep her aunt's counsel, but the minute he began speaking, interrupted him with a " Yes, I know," that rather dismayed him, for a moment. However, he had so much to say on the subject, and she had so little, that he managed to get the lead again, and to keep it. On the whole, Freda conducted herself pretty well, and came off with flying colours, though it was " mair luck than gude guidance," as the Scotch proverb says, that she did so. Lionel's delusions about her and her feelings were too deeply seated to be easily destroyed, and the rose-colour of the first stage of happy love covered and concealed everything that it was not desirable should see the light ; and as Freda had not the least idea that he had any delusions about her at all, she did not attempt to undeceive him, as, to do her justice, she certainly did the minute she made the discovery, but that unfortunately was not till after marriage.

Their intercourse, during the ten days before they were married, was not intimate or frequent. Freda was kept busy by her aunt "getting her things," and Lionel was obliged to run over to London for two or three days of the time, to arrange for a more lengthened absence. When they were together the mixture of simplicity and quickness in her conversation enchanted him, and if she dropped a few words he would rather she had not uttered, he immediately concluded either that she had *not* uttered them, or that she meant something quite different, and the fault was his in not understanding her. The fault was always his, not hers. Freda had a very retentive memory ; what

little she had learned, she remembered perfectly, and she had the dates of everything
at her fingers' ends. She went by the name
of the Major's Almanac at home, and her
uncle had great pride and amusement in
showing her off to her lover. She had been
very fond of poetry too, from quite a child,
had read all she could lay her hands on, and
remembered the musical swing of the words,
after reading them two or three times, without taking any trouble about learning them
by heart, and often only for the sake of their
musical swing, and not really understanding
their meaning, which seemed to her a matter
of secondary importance compared with their
sound. Mr. Fane was very fond of poetry
too, and charmed to find how their tastes
agreed. Her singing also he thought delicious, though untaught, and promised her
a first-rate master. In fact, she was to have
masters in everything. Native talent un-
trained was just what he had discovered he
most desired. Was he not to form her
mind ?

And so they were married.

Freda looked divinely beautiful and innocent in her bridal attire ; crowds of people attended the church at Cowes, merely to look at her, as her great beauty and early engagement had made a sensation in the neighbourhood. The long white veil and snowy flowers became her wonderfully, and her loveliness was something to astonish. She looked scarcely more than a child, and her composure was pronounced to be the sweetest thing ever beheld. Pure and fresh as a bit of exquisite painted china, there was a slightly surprised look in her face that men raved about ; and Lionel Fane was declared by an admiring congregation to be the luckiest fellow in the world.

And so indeed he considered himself to be, as he drove off from the church door, in a chaise and four, with his beautiful bride by his side. They were to go to the Highlands of Scotland for a week, and then meet the Camerons at Liverpool, and say good-bye, before the well-satisfied uncle and aunt sailed for Jamaica, after which they would have to enter on home life in Eaton Square at once.

It was then that Mr. Fane began his task

of developing his wife's heart and forming her mind—a task which he considered and expected to be one of the most delightful in the world.

But Mrs. Fane did not agree with him. She had not married with the slightest intention of having her heart developed or her mind formed. On the contrary, she had married with the idea of being given her own way in everything, and doing exactly what she liked.

Mr. Fane was in love.

Mrs. Fane was not.

And therein Mrs. Fane had an immense advantage over Mr. Fane.

Mr. Fane was first puzzled, then disappointed, then annoyed, and then furious.

For some time, in everything that went wrong, in everything that puzzled, in everything that disappointed him, he blamed himself and not his wife.

After that he blamed his wife and not himself, but made allowances for her, and was indulgent and patient.

And then he became furious.

This was when he discovered that she had

never loved him, did not love him, did not intend to love him, and did not wish to love him.

Of all this she made no secret whatever, and was very much astonished that he had not been aware of it from the first.

It was after some weeks of utter misery, and fatally frequent quarrels, that he left her, ostensibly to visit a friend, but in reality to take counsel with himself, and endeavour to see what there was that could be done. Calm consideration he felt was impossible, while in the same house with Freda. Still in love with her, and nearly driven mad by her beauty and her behaviour, he came home determined to expect less, to forbear more, and to put things, if possible, on a *better*, even though, as he sadly told himself it would be, a *lower* footing. And he came home to find her—gone.

With what followed, the reader is already acquainted.

Lionel Fane's character was a fine though a faulty one. He was a clever man, with deep feelings and strong passions ; but he was, it must be confessed, stern, vehement, and unforgiving. If men would sometimes let women choose them, instead of their choosing women, might it not be better for them? Maud Underwood, meek, tender, and sentimental, would have brought into his life that repose and calmness which it wanted. She would never have opposed, she would always have indulged him. Alas! he slighted Maud, and he adored Freda. He never discovered Maud's devoted affection of many years' standing, and he believed that in a week he had made Freda in love with him, and that it was only her exquisite childlike innocence that prevented her love from being before marriage all it would become afterwards. He was blind to what did exist, and saw in vivid colouring that which had no existence at all.

On the eve of his wedding-day, he wrote, as has been said, to his friend Mr. Underwood, and told him he was going to be married, after a very short acquaintance, to a beautiful, clever, and delightful girl, who was all, and more than all, he had ever imagined or wished his wife to be. He was not a man who ever wore his heart on his sleeve, and he said no more than that. He wrote not a word of the romantic manner in which he had first met her, but the letter, short as it was, breathed love and joy in every line, and Lewes felt assured that his friend was going to be perfectly happy.

During the three months of his married life, he only heard from Lionel once. The note he then received was short, dry, and uninteresting. It startled and shocked Mr. Underwood, not from anything that it contained, but from its containing nothing; and on it Maud founded the idea that the man she loved was not happy, which in her night-wanderings she had confided to Freda. The other idea, that she had been actually herself engaged to him, was one that had haunted her in her fever, and which still occasionally returned to her in those weary, dreary night hours that were supposed to be devoted to sleep. She had never really persuaded herself that he had not loved her, or that all the sweet silly talk between her mother and herself, in the dear old days, had been really founded on nothing—had really been only the baseless fabric of a dream.

And when she had reason to believe that his marriage was an unhappy one, a pale sickly romance sprang up in her mind, to torment her or to console her as the case might be : a romance that portrayed him as taken in, as marrying a girl he did not love, and as looking back to her and the days when he loved her with the fondness of regret.

She was dreaming a dream of this kind, yearning to be his friend, and to comfort him, when Lewes returned to her after having escorted Freda to Roseberry Farm. A sorrowful walk had Lewes Underwood that night. His pace was slow, his head was bent, he seemed to himself to be living years in every minute of time, and as if each step he took on the solid earth beneath his feet left youth, hope, and joy farther and farther behind him. Youth, hope, and joy, all buried in Roseberry Farm. Then he reproached himself for his selfishness in thinking his own thoughts, or dreaming his own dreams for a moment, while his friend and his friend's wife were in such a dreadful position. Hope and joy at Roseberry Farm ! What hope or joy was there for Freda now ?

A wife who had deserted her husband, who had deserted her husband and had been cast off by him ! And when he thought of Lionel, his spirit groaned within him in the bitterness of his grief. He knew his friend well, he knew his faults and his virtues, and he felt how both faults and virtues stood up in fatal array against any chance of his happiness.

His was indeed a noble life, wrecked by a woman.

And with this thought in his heart, he entered the little drawing-room, where, in the dim melancholy twilight, Maud lay on her invalid couch, dreaming of the same life.

CHAPTER II.

EXPLANATIONS.

MAUD UNDERWOOD received the Vicar with a smile as she always did. It would be a cloudy day, indeed, on which Maud had not a smile for her brother.

"You have been a long time out," she said, but not plaintively, for, fed by her sentimental fancies, she had not found the lonely hours tedious. "And that strange, dear girl has not been here either."

"No," replied he, catching thankfully at the opening; "I took her back to Roseberry Farm."

"Did you? Oh, I am sorry! But I suppose it was necessary for some reason."

"Yes; it was very necessary. I was obliged to do it. Maud, I have something extraordinary to tell you."

But at this Maud gave a sort of shiver.

"Oh, please don't, Lewes—unless you must; hearing extraordinary things makes me nervous always, since I was ill."

"I am afraid I must, dear. I think you would not be pleased if I did not tell you."

"Very well," she replied submissively. "I am listening, Lewes."

And she sank back on her couch with a pale, worn look that did not seem as if she was fit to bear anything.

"That girl—you thought her odd—did not you, Maud?"

"I thought her very *nice*—but I suppose she was odd."

"Nice!" cried the Vicar, with an impatient sigh. "Well, the fact is, Maud, she was only masquerading here. She is a lady."

"A lady! Dear me! And she sat in the kitchen, and she waited at table. Oh, my dear Lewes, she could not be a lady."

" She was masquerading, Maud."

" Masquerading !"

" Yes ; she had come down to visit Mrs. Dowlas—a sort of a humble friend, you know —and she had put on that dress for fun ; and I"—here he felt astonishment at himself for having been such a blockhead and spoke bitterly—"*I* took her for a servant, and so she pretended to be one."

" How very odd !" cried Maud, really interested, and sitting upright on her couch in the excitement of the interest she felt ; " how very, very odd !"

Here there was a pause ; and then Miss Underwood suddenly asked :

" And who is she, Lewes ?"

Here there was another pause, which at length the Vicar broke with slow reluctant speech.

" That is the very thing," he said ; " *that* is what I have got to tell you. In the first place, she is married !"

" Oh, Lewes ! that girl—that child—it is impossible ! Somebody is making game of you. She *can't* be married !"

" She is !"

" I am so tired !" said Maud, leaning back languidly on her couch ; " I wish you would tell me all about it, without making me ask."

This was not promising.

" I am telling you all about it," he answered fretfully, " only you won't let me."

Maud looked at him astonished, and the poor Vicar felt thoroughly ashamed of himself.

"We know something of her," he said ; " we know who she is."

" *I* don't," replied Maud ; " and if you do, you won't tell me."

" I will, Maud," said he very seriously and gently. " She is the wife of our friend—she is Lionel Fane's wife."

Maud screamed in what seemed a sort of terror :

" Lionel Fane's wife !"

Then there was silence between them for more than a minute. And then Maud sat up on her couch, white and agitated, speaking with difficulty, but with a gleam of joy in her eyes.

" He sent her here," she cried ; " he was

not happy—he thought we might do her good—he *sent* her here."

And there was a ring in her voice, exulting yet inexpressibly sad.

" No, no," cried he ; " she knew nothing of us—she had never heard of us—she ran away."

Maud sank back again as if utterly over-powered, and her brother feared for a moment she was going to faint.

Then she said in a weak voice :

" She ran away—she is wicked—we have been harbouring a bad person——"

" No, no, no !" interrupted he loudly and angrily ; " nothing of the sort—you *must* know it is nothing of the sort—you ought not to say such things. They were unhappy to-gether—many married people are—most, I dare say, if we only knew. He went on a visit from home, and she came to see her friends at the farm without telling him, and——"

" Her friends at the farm ? Oh, then she is *not* a lady !" interrupted Maud in her turn.

Never had Lewes Underwood felt so pro-voked, so irritated with his sister. It seemed to him that by everything she said, she was trying more and more to aggravate him. It was with the greatest difficulty that he kept his temper down and answered her without showing what he felt; but to his invalid sister, whose youth had not been happy, he never allowed himself to say a cross word.

"She *is* a lady—you must see that she is," he replied. "If she is not one, I wonder who is! Mrs. Dowlas was a humble friend. I think she must have been staying there for change of air or something, before our time"— here he stopped suddenly and gave a sigh, but he did not know why. "And so she came there very naturally as you *must* see; and all the rest has been merely accident."

"Accident!" said Maud faintly; "oh, poor Lionel!"

"He must have been to blame himself," said Lewes stoutly—"he must be in fault; there are faults on both sides—there always are—you know there always are."

Then Maud grew excited.

"We know him," she cried resentfully, "and we don't know her."

"She is all beauty and sweetness," said he.

" I am *sure* a man who took the right way could do anything with her."

" As if beauty *could* have anything to do with it !" answered his sister.

Then there was a little silence between them ; the Vicar, feeling inclined to be unreasonable and to be unreasonably annoyed with Maud, felt that it was best he should hold his tongue.

She lay back on her couch very white and worn-looking, her eyes too bright, and her lips a little apart. At last she said :

" How did you find it all out ?"

" He wrote to me that his wife had left him, and I found out he was under a mistake about—something ! And then he came, and they met——"

" He came !" cried Maud ; " he has been here !"

" Yes ; and saw her !"

" He has been here !" repeated Maud, her head falling back and her eyes closing, and she had a feeling in her heart as if the world had come to an end.

" He came here ; and we were talking it over when *she* appeared, and they recognised each other. Oh, Maud, it was such a scene!"

"Scene, indeed!" repeated she vaguely. "It is *all* scenes."

I don't know what she meant by this, nor did she; but I believe it seemed to her as if some fierce life-tragedy was being acted before her eyes, and that it was impossible that she was only a spectator. Then the brother and sister talked the whole business over, till Maud began to understand better what had happened.

"But why did you take her back to Roseberry Farm?" she cried; "that was such a mistake. It is so much better that she should be here—so much more natural. Are not you her husband's oldest friend?"

The Vicar felt and looked sheepish. What reason could he give Maud for this? How could he answer her why? He could not tell her that it was impossible for him to give his friend's wife a shelter in his house, because he had asked his friend's wife to marry himself, and his friend knew it.

"We all thought it best she should go there," he answered very awkwardly.

"And you were all wrong," answered Maud with unusual acrimony; "so like men! Why it is even more *respectable* that she should stay here than live with her inferiors; and, though he did not send her"—here she sighed—"still I think I could do her good. I should *like* to do her good."

"I am afraid it would not *do*," replied the Vicar, hanging his head.

"Not *do!*" cried she. "Oh, then there *is* something against her. She *has* done wrong. Oh, poor Lionel! Oh, poor, poor Lionel!"

She wrung her hands together, and sitting up, almost rose from her couch, and stood on her useless untried feet, in a restless agitation, to which repose was impossible.

Her brother went hastily to her, and carefully arranged her on her couch again.

"No, no, indeed no—nothing of the sort," he said; "it is impossible, and it is *not*. She is as innocent as a child, and her faults are only a child's faults. She is purity itself. But you are ill, and she is very young; it would not do—it would never do; and Mrs. Dowlas is her friend; she is to stay there for the present. It will be good for her, and we thought it the best arrangement—for the present, you know—something else will be done by-and-by, but for the present."

The Vicar spoke with unusual volubility, heaping up one reason upon another, and feeling more ashamed of himself as he did so, than perhaps he had ever felt in the whole of his life before.

But Maud proved unusually obstinate— unusually determined that her view of the matter was the right one.

" You are a clergyman, and his friend, and I am old, and can be of use to her," she persisted in saying ; " it will be best for her and for him ; and if people talk about their separation it will sound much better, a great deal better, for her to be at the Vicarage instead of the farm."

And she talked on till her brother was reduced to say : " Very well, we shall see about it ; something may be done. She is coming to you the day after to-morrow."

" Why not to-morrow ?" asked Maud, with complaint in her voice.

" I don't know," he said. " Oh yes, I was afraid it would be too much for you ; the excitement and surprise—you know how ill you have been—you have seen no one since your illness, and I thought you should have a day's rest before seeing her?"

"Why should seeing her tire me?" asked Maud. "And I feel perfectly well; I have not felt so strong for months."

And as she spoke she fainted away.

Poor Lewes Underwood! He had no Freda with her gentle movements and deft busy fingers to help him now. He had to do the best he could for his sister, and cook was his only auxiliary. But Sarah fortunately returned home while they were busy about the invalid, took her in hand, and after she had recovered her senses, put her to bed.

"If you are not better to-morrow, I shall send for Higgins," said her brother, as with a kind kiss he wished her good night.

"I am quite well," replied Maud; but she tossed about in feverish sleeplessness all night. Her mind wandered, she talked in a rambling, foolish way, and was agonised by recollections of the past.

"Then, from my couch may heavenly might
Keep those worst phantoms of the night.

> Again return the scenes of youth,
> Of confident, undoubting truth :
> Again his soul he interchanged
> With friends whose hearts were long estranged.
> They come in dim procession led,
> The cold, the faithless, and the dead,
> As warm each hand, each brow as gay,
> As if they parted yesterday."

In the middle of the night Lewes was summoned to his sister's bedside, and by daybreak the doctor was there also. He relieved Mr. Underwood's mind by saying that she was only feverish, there was nothing to be alarmed at ; it was one of those trifling relapses to which such a recovery as hers was subject, and she required nothing but quiet and rest to set her up again ; he gave her a soothing draught, and half an hour afterwards Maud Underwood was comfortably asleep.

" And a little dark liquid in a wine-glass does more for us—more for our minds, not for our bodies," soliloquised the Vicar, as he paced the garden walk, his heart relieved of its anxiety, " than all our prayers, all our resolutions, all our thoughts and wishes can do. We cannot quiet our own minds by the most violent mental efforts, but a little dark liquid in a wine-glass does it for us in a minute."

Foolish Vicar! do not, pray, draw any unpleasant conclusions from this fact; it is only because our minds affect our bodies, and the little dark liquid curing the body, *it* reacts upon the mind, and sleep follows.

The cool air and pleasant sunshine soon refreshed the Vicar's body, and through it his mind; and while the one is the case of the other, this must always be so. And he felt indescribably idle, while his vague thoughts, fixing nowhere, kept him easy and comfortable.

"There is nothing like a garden," he mused; "nothing like a garden on a summer day—nothing." And as he mused he came suddenly upon the straight rows of peas, where some branches were bare, and some drooped, heavy with their pods. Then it all rushed back upon him. He saw Freda in her exquisite grace and beauty, endowed from the top of her shining head to the sole of her fairy foot with piquant charms. He saw her standing there in as vivid colours as

if it were indeed she, and not a mere phantom
of his brain—her basket in one hand, the
other playing with the pea-pods, while he
stood face to face with her, and with beating
heart broached the idea that she might go to
school. Rest, peace, refreshment—vague, idle,
unfixed thoughts, were all gone—gone perhaps for the day; he was alive again, and his
life was a battle.

And where and how was the battle to be
fought? Not here, in all the dreary beauty
of the summer day—not here, on a spot that
must be for ever haunted by Freda—not in
idleness and rest. "Work, work, work," said
the Vicar; "thank God for work!" And he
turned briskly round, threw back his chest,
breathed frankly, and marched out of the
sweet sunny air, laden with blossom scents,
from the lazy hum of happy insects and the
delicious melody of birds, into the privacy of
his own study.

He walked straight up to his table, sat
down in his chair, dipped the pen resolutely
in the ink, and opening his sermon-book prepared to write. But when he opened his
sermon-book his eye instantly fell on the

sketch of two boxers eagerly fighting, and under them written in the free bold characters he knew full well :

" Always fighting. Never say die !"

He sprang indignantly to his feet, his whole face grew crimson with anger. " Incorrigible girl !" he cried, and made as if he would tear the insulted page from the book.

In doing so he again looked at the sketch. It was extremely clever, the whole effect given in half a dozen strokes, which could not have taken her two minutes to draw, and it was remarkably well done.

The humorous side of the affair now struck the Vicar for the first time; he held the book in his hands, and looking earnestly at the picture his eyes lit up with mirth, while he firmly compressed his lips to keep them steady and still. In vain. The sense of drollery in his nature overcame every other sense ; his risible muscles gave way, and he fairly roared with laughter.

He laughed loud and long ; after which he felt a great deal better.

Then he sat down again, and removing the page from the book, placed it in his desk, after having first copied the sentence from the top on to the next page, *without* copying the illustration of that sentence. This done, he set hard to work on his sermon, and did not leave it for four hours, when he was called to dinner. He set himself to look out in the Bible every text that in any way bore on his subject; to compare them together, to make sure about other translations that might be made of any word in any of them, and then to draw his lesson from the whole. It was a learned sermon, and a sermon full of careful examination and original thought; a sermon that required a man's whole mind to be brought to it, and which bore in itself the evidence that a man's whole mind *had* been brought and an undivided attention given.

The Vicar ate his dinner with some appetite, and felt pleased with himself.

It was in the evening of that day that a special messenger brought him a letter from Lionel Fane. His heart sank a little when he saw it. He knew he must read it; he knew that the reading must unsettle his mind, and leave him with a good deal to do over again. He felt like the well-known snail, who climbed up five feet every day and fell down four feet every night. "But never mind," he said bravely, "the wall was only twenty feet high, and the snail got to the top of it at last. I shall climb my twenty-feet wall also, in time. This is only part of the battle."

Then he read his letter, which was as follows:

"DEAR UNDERWOOD,

"I leave England to-night. Crawford, my lawyer, will write to you. I wish Mrs. Fane to remain at Roseberry Farm till she hears from Major Cameron, to whom I have written. Crawford will supply her with *necessary* money *till* she is placed with her uncle, when he will make her a proper allowance. When I die she will be a rich woman; till then I hope my name will never be heard of in England, as I hope no English name may reach me where I go. I have been a fool and a madman, but I am sane now. Farewell.

"Yours affectionately,

"LIONEL FANE."

23—2

Then Lewes Underwood repeated his sister's words : "Poor Lionel! poor, poor Lionel!" Adding to them : "Such a noble life wrecked by a woman. Oh, child, you have much to answer for! Will your heart and conscience ever, *ever* awake?"

CHAPTER III.

FAREWELL !

UNFORTUNATELY Dr. Higgins was mistaken, as the cleverest doctors sometimes are, in his opinion, and before the night of that day Maud Underwood was dangerously ill; so ill, indeed, that it appeared as if human skill could not avail to keep her back from that heaven of perfect bliss, that land where there are no more tears, " where the wicked cease from troubling, and the weary are at rest," from which our most earnest endeavours, the most eager efforts of our lives are directed, to draw our beloved ones, if they take even a fitful step or two towards it; and if they

draw near its lonely confines, then our endeavours and our efforts redouble themselves,
and our agony is great.

Mr. Underwood was obliged to visit those
of his parishioners who might perchance also
lie in deadly sickness, and he was obliged to
perform his Sunday duties as usual, to go
through those services with calmness and
deliberation, in which now and again a prayer,
or here and there a versicle, came home to
his heart with a force, and stirred it into an
emotion, that he had never found in them
before. Had these beautiful services verily
and indeed till now been as dead corpses to
him, and was it death that was for the first
time giving them life? He shuddered at the
idea even while he calmly read the words,
and was to the eyes of the congregation a
calm and decorous clergyman.

He had no time to go to Roseberry Farm.
He had, almost, no time to think of Freda.
She came to the Vicarage the day he had
appointed, but she only saw Sarah, who told
her that Miss Underwood was ill, and the
Vicar could not see her, so Freda had to go
home again, and no meeting took place

between them.   On the fourth day Maud was better, on the fifth the doctor pronounced her to be out of danger ; she smiled and spoke like herself; and on the evening of the sixth day the Vicar walked down to Roseberry Farm.

He jumped over a stile and crossed a field, which brought him, by a short cut, to the farm-yard ;.but he was not destined to reach his destination in a hurry.   It was milking-hour, and in that field a girl was milking a very pretty brown and white dapple cow, and singing gaily as she milked her

MILKMAID'S SONG.

" Cows softly lowing
      'Neath rosy skies,
Buttercups blowing
      Under my eyes ;
Birds singing o'er me
      Recklessly sweet,
Summer before me,
      Spring at my feet ;
Breezes delicious
      Fluttering by,
Cloudlets capricious
      Flecking the sky.
Daylight is going,
      Gladly I see
Cows softly lowing,
      Waiting for me."

Freda rose from her stool as she finished her song, and turning round suddenly, faced the Vicar. A glad look came into her eyes when she saw him, and she nodded her head at him in a friendly manner, while she dipped a mug into the milk-pail and handed it to him, dropping a pretty little curtsey as she did so. Her dress seemed to him picturesque; buttercups were stuck in posies about her large straw hat, under which her beauty shone out fairer and brighter than ever.

From the atmosphere of that sad sick-room, from the melancholy wanderings of its inmate, from the life he had led therein for the last five days—seeming, in its dreary monotony, like as many weeks when he looked back on it—he stepped at once into a graceful idyl, wherein earth and its inhabitants remained what a beneficent Creator had intended them to be, till, through the folly of man, sin and sorrow were forced in. O freedom! O freshness! what gifts can make up for your loss? Then the thought struck him like a blow. Was it by the folly of a *man* the change was wrought? Alas! no, it was by a *woman*, and he looked at Freda and sighed.

"Is she better?" cried she, her cheek paling a little, and an anxious light dimming her sweet eyes.

He smiled, pleased at her earnestness.

"Oh yes," he said, "she is better; she is recovering, thank God!"

He spoke the last two words very reverently, and Freda's young cheek grew paler yet.

"Has she been so ill as *that*?" she cried, appalled by his thankfulness.

He did not ask her "as what?" or attempt to point a lesson. His whole being was refreshed, merely by her presence in the cool summer twilight, and he was in no mood for preaching. He only repeated the words, "She is recovering."

"When may I come and see her?" asked Freda, reassured.

He shook his head. "I don't know; not for some time; she is not fit for visitors."

"It must be soon, or not at all," replied she with decision. "I am thinking of going away."

"Going away!" he cried, startled. "Where Why?"

"It's nice," she said—"of course it's nice—
it always is at Roseberry Farm, but it's not
what it was when the old people were at
home, and we were all lads and lassies.
Letty's busy; she *has* to be busy, but she
can't help it; and Jack—Jack's a dear, but
he's a married dear now, and a wee bit heavy
on hand. He thinks so much of cattle and
pigs, and of course I don't care *very* much for
pigs; but Letty does. I was *delighted* with
them the first day, and quite thought about
pigs, but somehow it doesn't last."

She spoke almost apologetically, as if inclined to blame herself, and looking for
excuses, and then laughed at him with sparkling eyes and dimpling chin.

"But you cannot have heard from your
uncle," he said. "You had better stay here
till you do. In fact, where can you go?"

"I have heard from nobody," she said,
"except one nasty lawyer—and he came
himself—*such* a nasty one! But he gave me
some money, and he said he should pay Letty
ten pounds a month as long as I stayed.
Fancy paying for my keep, just as if I were
a horse."

"Oh, you have seen Mr. Crawford. Did he tell you anything of—your husband?"

Freda clapped her hands.

"Yes; he's gone to the other side of the world—really gone, and I am as free as air!"

She looked as free as air as she stood before him, and there was an indefinable charm in that airy freedom that went straight to his heart.

"I am thinking of going to school," she said. "It was *your* idea, you know, and it isn't a bad one. I've an immense deal I could do there, and I *think* I should like the girls. I never knew a girl except Letty, and I dote upon *her*. It would be decidedly new to go to school."

"I suppose it might be managed," he replied thoughtfully.

"Anything can be managed," said Freda promptly. "I've money, and I'm free!"

"You would not be free at school," he said. "I don't know how you would like the long hours and the confinement and the rules; but I'll tell you what, they take boarders at schools—parlour boarders they

call them, I think—who are received on dit-
ferent terms, have lessons from the masters,
and join in the studies only when they
choose. I think you might go as a parlour
boarder, and that it might not be a bad plan."

" Thank you kindly, sir, for all your information," cried she with a laughing curtsey.
" Why, it's *settled*, and I'm going to be
one."

Then she took a letter out of her pocket
and flourished it in the air, so as almost to
touch his eyes.

" Why don't you read ?" she cried. " What
are eyes made for ?" And she burst into a
sweet ringing laugh.

He caught the letter from her hand and
read :

" DEAR MADAM,

" We shall be happy to receive you
here, but we think under the peculiar circumstances that it would be more conducive to
your comfort that you came as a parlour
boarder than as a pupil. In that case you
would have all the comforts and pleasures of
a home in a private family, with the advan-

tages of masters and the society of any of the
young ladies you wish to associate with. The
terms will be £150 per annum, exclusive of
washing, or £175 if you choose to have a
private sitting-room. I will give all particulars in my next letter, but, meantime, you
will, I am sure, quite understand my asking
you to send me a reference. Hoping to hear
from you by return of post,

" Believe me, dear madam,
" Yours truly,
" L. BRIGGS."

" I want to go because she calls me
' dear madam.' She *must* be fun to call *me*
'madam!' But what in all the wide world
does she mean by a reference ? What *is* a
reference, Mr. Underwood ? And can I send
it by post ?"

" I'm a reference," replied he, laughing.

" Well, I can't send you by post."

" No; but I can write to your Mrs. or Miss
Briggs, and tell her all about you. A clergyman is always a safe reference. She wants
to hear who you are from some one besides
yourself."

"That is rather mean, I think," said Freda calmly.

"Who is she? and what made you write to her?"

"She advertised in the *Times*, and I answered it," replied she rather loftily, as if she felt the importance of the position.

"You must show me the advertisement, and I will reply to her letter, and ask for *her* references, and see that it is all right before you go a step further."

"That's the worst of telling men anything," said Freda discontentedly. "You never get a chance afterwards; they take it all out of your hands, and act for you."

"And if it is a desirable place for you to go to, we might arrange for one quarter, and you might stay there till Major and Mrs. Cameron write about your going out to them."

"To Jamaica? Ah! it would have been better if I had gone with them at once. What a goose my aunt was! It's odd how right I always am; but she had it her own way, and *made* me marry him."

"Poor fellow!" said Mr. Underwood.

"Why do you pity *him*?" cried Freda, astonished. "It's *me*!"

"Yes, it's you; but it's him too. You think only of yourself. He is one of my oldest and best friends. His marriage has made him miserable, and banished him from his home, perhaps for ever."

"Oh, I hope so!" she cried. "You don't think there's a *chance* of his ever coming back, do you?"

"Scarcely," replied he dryly. "He is very determined."

"That's all right," said Freda; "but I declare you frightened me for a moment."

As Mr. Underwood walked home, he felt his heart, somehow or other, was relieved of a great weight, and a great weight of a kind that it was very little accustomed to bear. His healthy, manly nature answered to the first touch of conscience, and whilst standing there conversing with lovely, radiant Freda, and even when he had passed out of her enchanting presence, he felt no aching in his heart, no feeling that he could not have wished to have felt towards the girl who was his friend's wife. If he had not been able,

while talking and looking at the childlike
creature, to think of her consciously all the
time as of a wife, still he *had* had a conscious
feeling that she had gone out of his reach,
and that she was not, and never could be,
any part or portion of his life. He breathed
freely and stretched his arms out gladly as he
walked along, and this fact became keenly
visible to him. Then he raised his eyes up
to the skies, lifted his hat from his head, and
said, " Thank God !"

If she had been free, what would he have
felt ? If she was free to-morrow ? He put
the thought vehemently down ; but he sighed
as he did so.

Ah, Lionel ! best friend. Poor Lionel !
with your ruined hopes, and shattered household gods—a homeless wanderer on the earth.
Your friend is true and loyal to you as friend
can be ; but he is only a man after all. He
is a good man though, and a good man is a
great creation ; and he is a good man, not
trusting in his own goodness or in his own
strength.

Mr. Underwood wrote to Mrs. Briggs, and
heard from her in return ; the correspondence

was satisfactory, as also were his communications with Mrs. Brigg's references, and on the subject of terms with the "nasty" lawyer, Mr. Crawford. In fact, the whole thing was arranged more quickly than might have been expected. Lewes longed, both on his own account and on hers, to have Freda safely away, settled at what appeared to be a good school; "and then," he said to himself frankly, " then I shall return to the old life again."

The old life. Yes, then he could return to the old life. But would it be the old life? Would it really be just the same life it was before he found Freda in the wood? or would it be a new life, bearing its date from the moment when he brought her thence under the stars into his home?

How long ago that night seemed to him now—how very long ago!

Freda went to school before Miss Underwood was well enough to see her; but the girl insisted on seeing Miss Underwood.

" I like her," she said, " and I won't go away without looking at her sweet pale little face—I won't! Get me into her room while she's asleep."

"Get you into the room while she's asleep!" repeated Lewes doubtfully.

"If there's one thing I hate, it's any one repeating my words," cried Freda, snapping him up. "It's so silly. *Very* few things are worth saying once, and *nothing's* worth saying over again. Of course, you'll take me into her room while she's asleep. What's the matter now? Wasn't I her servant? Didn't I sleep in her room, and attend on her in the night? I'll tell you what, young man—you'll never make your way in the world if you create difficulties about trifles."

The Vicar laughed.

"Well," he said, "we'll see what can be done. Come down about five o'clock in the afternoon—that is when she sleeps soundest, I think—and I'll see what can be done."

"Yes," replied she, "and *I'll* see what can be done also."

She made her appearance, bright and smiling, at the Vicarage even before the appointed hour; and she followed the Vicar into his sister's room with a play of walking on tiptoe, and hushing herself and everybody else besides, indescribably pretty.

Then as she stood at the bedside and looked at the sleeping face on the pillow, her own grew a little pale, and she turned reproachful eyes on the Vicar. To his great surprise, she raised one rosy little finger in the air, and made a sign above the sleeping woman's head, which he saw was, and could be only, the sign of the cross. It was instantaneous—over almost as it commenced; and Lewes felt that strange sensation the next instant, contradicting his own senses, and telling him he could not have seen it, that she had not done it, which is sometimes experienced with painful vividness after we have witnessed a thing equally rapid and impossible. Freda could not have made the sign of the cross in the air over his sister.

"Why did you do that?" he said in a whisper, as they quitted the room, too impatient for a solution of the mystery to wait.

But she looked indignantly at him, pointed to the bed they were leaving behind them, and said almost ostentatiously, "Hush!"

He felt reproved and abashed, and waited till they were at the foot of the stairs. Then he repeated the question aloud:

24—2

" Why did you do that ?"

"What ?" she asked innocently.

He raised his finger, and imitated exactly her gestures in the air made a few seconds before.

Freda burst out laughing.

" Oh !" she cried ; " you can do it too, can you !"

" What made you do it ?   Who taught you ?" almost angrily.

" An old servant always did it at me every night when I was a child, and she thought I was asleep.   I haven't thought of it for years, and I've not the least notion why I thought of it then.   I don't believe I did.   I don't remember thinking of it or *intending* to do it. 1 *did* it—I believe, in fact, that *I* didn't do it at all ; it was my finger."   She held up the pretty rose-tipped little thing, and, examining it with attentive eyes, showed it to him, and asked very gravely, " Isn't it odd ?"

" Yes, it *is* odd," he said.   " And was that nurse of yours a Roman Catholic ?"

" I have not the least idea," replied Freda. "It was ages upon ages ago ; I was a baby, I believe.   I don't think I recollect the woman a bit; and I'm sure I don't recollect her doing *that*. I think I must have invented it all—I don't suppose I ever had such a nurse. Only my finger did it while I stood there; and when you questioned me, the answer came, and I thought it was true while I said it, but I have not a notion whether it is now. How queer we are! Mr. Underwood, do *you* think we have lived before ?"

" Lived before ?"

" Yes. Bless the man ! is the idea new to him ?"

" Tell me what you mean by '*lived before?*'"

" Well, I think I was a bird; I am almost sure I was a bird. Do you think *you* were a bird, Mr. Underwood ? I used to believe that all women had been birds, and all men beasts. But I can't think you were ever a beast. Do you ? You *can't* have been *much* of a beast." And she looked at him approvingly.

Mr. Underwood laughed, but Freda was perfectly grave; and he turned to her with puzzled inquiry :

" Do you mean what you are saying ?" he asked.

"I don't know," she said, with a vague, empty look.

Mr. Underwood gazed earnestly at her, and then he sighed.

She raised her eyes to his, sparkling with life and animation; not the same creature she had been a moment before.

"It is no use," she cried; "there are things one never can make out. Why should one think of them? they are only vexing." And she laughed gaily; then stopped and said, "Hush! She will not hear me, will she? I *do* like her. I wonder why I like her so much; for I suppose she is a little insipid; is not she?"

"I am sure I don't know," replied the Vicar, rather awkwardly.

"Don't you?" cried Freda sharply. "How very odd!"

They walked out of the house in silence.

"I go to-morrow morning early," she said presently. "Jack takes me to the train, and somebody meets me. Won't it be funny? I am going to be my own mistress at last! Oh, I am glad I came here! Whatever one does always turns out rightly and for the best.

That is a very nice part of this world's arrangements, which one doesn't know of or expect when one is young. I hadn't a notion how my going to Roseberry Farm would turn out; and I was really frightened when I did it, which was silly, for I might have known. But, you see, I haven't much experience yet," she added apologetically. " I've more now even than I had then. I shall know better next time."

" Your coming here has caused your separation from your husband, and his leaving his home and his country," replied Lewes, with a good deal of meaning in his voice.

" Yes, exactly," she replied simply. " *So* nice ; *nothing* could be better !"

" Child !" cried the Vicar almost fiercely, " do you *never* think of any one but yourself ?"

She turned her astonished eyes upon him, and a look of pain came into their transparent depths. (Such wonderful eyes as they were !)

" Are you angry with me ?" she said softly. " What have I done ? Don't scold me this last little day."

The words " last little " were uttered in an irresistibly coaxing manner.

" No," he said, looking at her sadly. " What would be the use of scolding you ? You are blind ; you can't see. Time—time may open your heart ; for you are heart-blind, Freda—you are heart-blind. But if it does, what will you do ? and what will be the end of it all ?"

" But why should there be any end ?" she asked. " We shall go on living. Why should there be an end then, more than now ?"

And she laughed roguishly, as if she felt she had caught him in some very foolish mistake or slip of the tongue.

" Do you ever think of—death ?" said the Vicar ; but he paused and hesitated before he brought the last word out, seeming doubtful whether he had any *right* to say such a thing to this girl, as she stood before him, an embodiment in her fresh beauty of endless life.

The thought sprang up in his mind, without any call from him, " If I wished to *understand* eternity, there it is !" But this was only followed by the feeling of the horrors of *time*. Time, that could, would, and must bring to age, decrepitude, and decay even Freda—even Freda! Then the idea came vividly over him of Freda dead—Freda in her grave, before Time had worked his cruel will on that lovely form. But he shuddered at the knowledge of mortality, of the thought of Freda's form decaying in her grave. He shuddered, and for one moment put his hand before his eyes that he might shut out from them the exquisite reality which had given rise to the dreadful vision—not of what might, but what must be.

When he withdrew his hand, he found the gay girl was laughing in his face.

"Death!" she said. "No; I never think of death. Why should I? We are none of us going to die—are we? I'm not, for one; and, if I were you, I wouldn't either."

"Don't talk so lightly," was the reply. "You are not such a child but what you must *know* you ought not to talk so. Death may come to me or to you at any minute—at this very minute it might come."

"Only it won't," said she coolly. "You can't frighten me that way, Mr. Clergyman." Then she paused and afterwards clapped her hands, and cried, with a little air of triumph: "There! it didn't! How could you be so silly? Now aren't you disappointed?" And she laughed gleefully.

"It is no use talking to you—" he began, and she saucily interrupted him by saying:

"Not a bit, not one bit of use; so *don't* talk, there's a dear."

Then she stopped, laughed again, and whether it was from the exertion of laughter (which, however, did not appear to be the least exertion to her), or a feeling of propriety, he could not tell, but a lovely rosy hue spread over her face as she cried: "I didn't mean to say that. Only you *are* one, and so, why shouldn't I?" And then she laughed again, a clear, ringing, childlike laugh, which at last compelled him to laugh too, in spite of himself, just as the laugh of children compels us to join our merriment to theirs, though we do not even know what has given rise to it. Then she nodded her head at him, pleased and friendly. "That's right," she cried approvingly, "I like to see you laugh. Oh, why are we not all, always laughing? It's our one advantage over beasts, you know. Why don't we use it oftener?"

He shook his head at her; but the healthy hearty laughter had dissipated his more serious thoughts, and he only said:

"That is a duty which at any rate *you* don't fail in, whatever we others may do."

"Ah!" she cried, "does that dear old thing ever laugh? Will she laugh when she gets well again? When *will* she get well? I can't think why people are ever ill—it's foolish. I never mean to be ill. What's the use of a soul if it can't keep its own body right? Oh, Mr. Underwood, have you heard from Professor Stubbs?"

He stared at her.

"Oh, come; you must remember. Don't be stupid. About that dream of hers, you know. The poetry dream—

"'That grantest wings
And voices to the woodland birds,
Grant me the power of saying things
Too simple and too sweet for words.'

Ah, there are so many things too sweet for

words to say, so many things words *can't* say. It is such a pity. I am always longing to invent a new way of talking that *can* express things. Perhaps that's what our faces are given us for."

And, in perfect simplicity, she turned hers upon him as she spoke.

He shrank back for a moment, then looked with his clear, honest eyes full into hers, and answered :

"My dear child, in heaven we shall all understand each other."

"And in heaven that dream shall be explained too," she cried; "for it shan't here. I know all about it. I could explain; but I won't—I won't—never—never—never."

They had reached the farm, and stood still, facing each other, on the threshold of the open door.

"Come in," she said imperiously.

"Not now," he answered calmly. "I saw you first under the open blue sky, and it is there I will bid you good-bye. God bless you, child! Send for me if you want a friend."

He looked full in her face as he spoke, and

held out his hand. She caught it in both
hers, pressed it in a childish, fondling way,
and, to his amazement, tears filled her eyes,
which glanced through them with extraordinary transparent brilliancy.

"I'll want a friend directly, if I may send
for you. Oh, I do like you so. I hate saying
good-bye. God bless you, too."

The last words fell with almost a solemn
sound, like the bright-striking bell in a little
church turret, and, as they fell, a blessing
seemed to steal into his heart.

He gently disengaged his hand from hers,
and, without another word or gesture, turned
from her and walked rapidly away.

When quite out of sight and hearing of
Roseberry Farm, he stopped. smiled, and
looked up at the open blue sky of which he
had spoken.

"Thank God!" he said; "Lionel, I can
meet you anywhere on earth or in heaven;
and, if the strength of man can do it, I will
win your wife back for you before we meet."

And so he went home.

CHAPTER IV.

AT SCHOOL.

IT is six months since we have seen Freda ; six months since she became an inmate of Mrs. Briggs' establishment. Six months is a long time : it is twenty-six weeks, or one hundred and eighty-four days ; one hundred and eighty-four days of schooling and discipline, and decorous, well-regulated life. What will all this have done for our wild, reckless Freda ? In what way, and how, will it have changed, softened, civilised her ? We shall see.

The scene is a long, comfortable room, used as schoolroom by the twelve young ladies and two teachers (French and English), who, with

the addition of one parlour boarder, are at
present the sole members of Mrs. Briggs'
establishment. The ages of the young ladies
vary from fourteen to seventeen, for it is a
distinguished finishing-school to which Freda
has put herself; and at the moment when we
introduce ourselves to it, they are all busy
with their studies. Mademoiselle Lacrox and
Miss Waring sit . at their respective desks,
and as all the scholars are engaged preparing lessons, silence reigns in the long,
comfortable room—silence of that profound
and peculiar kind that can only be felt where
there are a number of people. The hand of
the clock over the mantelpiece points to a
quarter to twelve ; an hour and a quarter,
therefore, must elapse ere the prisoners are
free for the recreation they enjoy before
dinner. An hour and a quarter is a very
long time when you may be only fourteen
years old, and are certainly not more than
seventeen, and that hour and a quarter is to
be spent in hard study. A few pairs of eyes
which have been directed towards the
chimney-piece clock, return with patient
endurance to their books, their owners seeing

only too plainly that there is no use in looking
at the clock yet.

Suddenly a change. The door opens, and
in glides a vision of youth, beauty, and freedom, her tiptoe steps scarcely seeming to
touch the ground, her cheeks full of roses,
her lips apart with the joyous smile that
shines as much in her splendid eyes, as on
them. It is Freda, scarcely changed since
we saw her—any change being that only of a
beauty that develops itself more as the girl
advances towards womanhood. Advances
towards, only ; for womanhood still looks far
enough from this " phantom of delight."

She pauses a moment and composes her
features, then a well-regulated, rather hollow
voice utters the following words, in studied
accents :

" My dear young friends, raise your eyes
from your studies for a moment. I have
something to say to you."

The lips are the lips of Freda, but the voice
is the voice of Mrs. Briggs.

Twenty-eight eyes look up astonished at
her, and fourteen mouths relax from gravity
into laughter, for the teachers laugh as much

as the scholars at the daring imitation of their head.

Then Freda resumes her own manner. She waves an embroidered handkerchief in the air above her head and shouts, if such sweet silvery accents can be called shouting, " A holiday ! a holiday ! a half-holiday is proclaimed ! O yes ! O yes ! O yes ! God save the Queen !"

And then she sings loudly half a verse of that National Hymn which you may remember she chanted to Letty when you first saw her :

> " Confound their politics,
>   Frustrate their knavish tricks,
>   God save the Queen !"

ending with a long trill, shake, and flourish on the last word.

" I like singing that, girls, don't you ? It's the only swearing I'm allowed, and it's better to sing swearing than to have no swearing at all. 'Confound their politics !' does not it rattle out nicely ? I *should* like to be a man to be able to confound things whenever I wanted ; I'm quite sure it is my nature to !"

" But the holiday, Freda ? the holiday ?" cried half a dozen, or perhaps a dozen fresh young voices; and Mademoiselle La Croix and Miss Waring looked as anxious as their pupils on the subject. Poor teachers! We always think of the children when the pleasures of a holiday are in question, but *what* are the few hours of freedom to them compared with what they are to those who teach them?

Then Freda sprang lightly on to a table, folded her little hands in front of her, and made a profound curtsey.

"I am eighteen to-day," she said in tones that seemed to sparkle with her eighteen years; "I am eighteen to-day, and there is a holiday."

"Hurrah!" cried two or three voices, and Freda, taking the hint, called emphatically for three cheers for Briggs, which were given with a will.

And then she sang, all following her voice in chorus—all? Yes, two elder voices, one with a foreign accent, might be detected through the *mêlée*:

> "For Briggs is a jolly good fellow, my boys,
> For Briggs is a jolly good fellow, my boys,
> For Briggs is a jolly good fellow, my boys,
> Hurrah, hurrah, hurrah!"

The chorus, never given with greater zest, echoed and re-echoed through the room. Freda finished it off with a pirouette on the table, and her example was immediately followed by a dozen pirouettes about the apartment, while the last hurrah still trilled on excited lips.

None of the performers in this little drama were aware that the door of the room had opened while they were in the middle of the third "Briggs is a jolly good fellow, my boys," or that a gentleman, ushered in by the maid, had been a silent and interested spectator of the scene.

Such was the case, however, and a manly voice, sounding very manly indeed amid all these shrill trebles, now made itself heard with the question, "Can I speak to Mrs. Fane for a few minutes?"

Mrs. Fane finished her pirouette facing him, and then casting up her hands, exclaimed, though not loud enough for him to actually distinguish the words, "Heavens! it's the nasty lawyer!"

She leaped to the ground with an airy lightness that suggested the idea of flying,

and advancing towards the door, while horri-
fied and embarrassed school-girls shrank back
on every side, she, perfectly mistress of the
occasion, extended her hand with queenly
grace, smiled with angelic sweetness, and
said : " How do you do, Mr. Crawford ?"
with a decorous coolness that *proved* it was
impossible she had been just before dancing
on the table, singing loudly the chorus of a
drinking song.

"Oh, Mrs. Fane !" cried the lawyer, losing
his presence of mind much more than she did ;
" I really beg your pardon."

" Don't mention it," replied Freda with an
air of indulgent patronage ; " I shan't think of
it again."

Then the lawyer composed his features
into a lugubrious gravity that the occasion
hardly seemed to call for, even when it was
remembered that the actors in it were a
lawyer and his client.

" Perhaps I may request a private interview, Mrs. Fane ?"

Miss Waring had now come to the rescue.

" I am very sorry, sir," she said, " that you
have been shown in here by mistake ; there

is a drawing-room for visitors where Mrs. Briggs would have been happy to receive any friend of Mrs. Fane's while the young lady was being sent for."

The lawyer bowed with unrelenting gravity.

"Thank you, madam," he replied, "but I inquired for Mrs. Briggs. I was informed that she had just gone out, and I followed the servant here, where she mentioned that I should find Mrs. Fane."

"And so he did," cried Freda to Miss Waring, "it's all right." Then she dropped Mr. Crawford a curtsey, and said sweetly, "At your service, sir."

Again the lawyer bowed gravely.

"I should wish to speak to you alone, madam."

Freda glanced round her. She caught one of the young lady's eyes and gave, what I had almost called an audible wink—it was such a very perceptible one; then she said with unruffled sweetness, "I don't mind witnesses."

"I do," said he with emphasis; "my business is private."

"Come along then," cried she briskly, and

losing the extreme civility of manner she had hitherto observed, "and don't be all day about it; I'm *very* busy, but I can spare you ten minutes."

And she tripped along the passage that led to the drawing-room, Mr. Crawford following her.

Arrived there, she poked the fire, making it blaze splendidly; looked at herself in the glass above it, laughed in her own pretty face, put her bow straight, and pushed her hair a little farther back from her forehead; then, thrusting her hands down deep into the pockets of her polonaise, and assuming a firm, determined, business-like air, she turned round upon the lawyer, and said, "Now then," in a voice and manner exactly like a man's.

"My business is of an unpleasant nature," began he.

"Oh, I know," said Freda, reassuming her natural sweetness and grace; "I'm very sorry, but I can't help it."

He looked at her with surprise.

"I can't, really. Don't scold about the money. I was obliged to spend it, and I do want more. A man's donkey died suddenly.

He was quite an old man. I was obliged to give him another. It died in the night, and he is really quite an old man. What could I do ? I *had* to get him a donkey. And then the other bill was just a black silk for Miss Waring. I really believe it was her lover she was expecting" (here she gave a little silvery laugh), "and she had nothing nice to wear—not a thing, and I saw she'd been crying ! Now, I could not help it, could I ?" quite coaxingly. And as he still looked imperturbably grave, she added a little impetuously : " I suppose you think a five-guinea silk would have done—much you men know about it ! It *had* to be a costume, or it wouldn't have been in time ; and the ten-guinea was the nicest of all, so I got that, and I *believe* she was as happy as a queen. He'd been away for years and years."

In reply to which long speech, Mr. Crawford only said in exactly the same serious manner that he had preserved throughout :

" It is *not* about money that I wish to speak to you to-day."

Freda stared in his face, and then laughed a little.

"What a goose I am," she cried, "to have told you all that! But I really thought you were going to scold me." Then she shrugged her little shoulders and said : " I *hate* being scolded." Having recovered from this fear, she put on her company manners again. "Sit down," she said, with polished ease. " Why are we standing ? What a season it has been—so cold, is not it ? Very bad for trade, I am afraid." She had not an idea whether a cold season was bad for trade, but she said it with a pretty little regretful air. " Now, *do* you like Salvini, or do you *not ?* To my mind he's perfect, but tastes are *so* different." And she regarded him with a sort of languishing question in her eyes, as if on his decision about Salvini's merits a good deal of her comfort depended.

Mr. Crawford cleared his throat ominously.

" Mrs. Fane," he said rather abruptly, " this is not a moment for small-talk. I have come to you about business."

"I'm *so* sorry," lisped Freda. "I *like* small-talk, and I *don't* like business."

"On very unpleasant business," persisted he.

" Worse and worse," lisped she.

" I am sorry to say that your husband——"

She interrupted him, putting up her two little hands as if to defend herself from some visible danger.

" Don't say it !" she cried. " Don't. He's *not*—coming home ?"

" No," said the lawyer quite solemnly ; " he is not coming home."

" Oh," she cried, " then I care for nothing."

He looked at her with strong disapprobation.

" You care for nothing but what concerns yourself," he said.

Something of the same sort, words to the same effect, came floating back to her on the wings of memory, spoken by a different voice in a different manner—words something like, " Child, do you never think of any one but yourself ?" and as they floated into her mind she gave a little sigh.

" Your husband," continued Mr. Crawford, " was at——"

" Stop !" interrupted Freda. " I don't care. I don't want to hear where he is. I had rather not. We have agreed not to hear about each other."

" For this once, have patience," replied he.
" Trust me, it will be the last time."

Light came into her eyes, and her lips
parted in a joyous smile.

" Ah, I am glad," she cried.   " Very well,
then ; I won't mind.   Say what you have to
say, and have done with it."

" You dislike him as much as ever ?" asked
her lawyer.

" I ?" cried Freda, astonished. " Of course.
I hate him."

She spoke as if she meant it, and he gazed
at her beautiful face with wonder and dis-
gust.   Then, to punish her heartlessness, he
said out, in abrupt, sudden words, the news
he had come with the intention of breaking to
her gently.

" Your husband is dead !" said he.

Freda looked straight at him, and then
burst out laughing.

" Oh yes, I dare say," she cried.   " Come
now, what is it ?   Tell me, really."

" Your husband is dead," repeated Mr.
Crawford in a loud voice.

" Dead !" she repeated.   " What nonsense !
Don't go on saying it, it's so silly, and I really

haven't time. It's a holiday, and we're going to amuse ourselves with a game of hunt-the-slipper. It's my birthday. I'm eighteen to-day." And she looked at him and smiled.

" It may be your birthday, and you may be eighteen to-day," replied the lawyer brutally; " but for all that, your husband, Lionel Fane, is dead—dead—dead !" And he repeated the word as if it gave him pleasure to do so.

" My husband, Lionel Fane, is dead—dead —dead !" reiterated Freda after him, but as if she did not take in the meaning of the words she uttered.

" Yes, he is dead. He died——"

" But it is impossible," cried she. " *Dead !* He is young—he is strong. He *can't* be dead."

" Do young, strong people never die ?" said the lawyer, with a tinge of bitterness in his voice and manner. " *I* lost a son, twenty-one years of age : he died in my arms."

A soft look of pity came into Freda's eyes. She stepped swiftly up to him, and her little hand touched his arm with light, friendly touch.

"Oh, what a pity!" she said. "I am *so* sorry."

He regarded her with cool surprise; then his manner softened a little towards this girl, who was mourning the dead son he had ceased to mourn long ago.

"It is three years since he died," he said, as if anxious to relieve *her*. "We have left off grieving; and as to you, you should be sorry for yourself."

Her whole air and manner changed. She was radiant as ever, laughing gaily.

"No, thank you," she cried, with a little curtsey. "I am not going to be sorry for myself—not just yet awhile, please. I'll wait till I am old and hunchy, if you don't mind." And she drew her slender figure up, and laughed at him.

"Your husband is dead," he answered sternly.

Then she gave a great start back, as if she *remembered* having heard the words before.

"Dead?" she said. "Oh no; that is impossible. He is not dead."

"He is. It *is* possible. He is dead. He

died—he was thrown from his horse and killed on the spot "

Freda shuddered all over. She was seized with a shivering fit, such a one as ushers in a fever; and she turned very white, and held out her hands, as if she wanted support and feared she was going to fall. She looked helplessly and beseechingly into the lawyer's grave face, with eyes that entreated him to contradict himself. Then she gave a strange, stifled scream, and uttered the words: "He *can't* be dead;" but not as if she believed them. It seemed now as if she thought he *was* dead, though she denied it.

"One would suppose nobody ever died," cried Mr. Crawford roughly. "Why should not he as well as another? He was always a wild rider, and he had had enough to make him ride recklessly. He was thrown from his horse—he is dead. You must just believe it and bear it as other women have had to believe and to bear the deaths of their husbands —aye, other women who, maybe, *loved* the men who died."

"I did not love him," said Freda, with a stony stare, and not knowing what she was saying; "I did not love him. I was glad he went; I never wanted to see him again. But *dead!* Oh, it is horrible! Oh, Mr. Crawford, do you *think* his soul is in heaven?"

"What do I know about souls in heaven, young lady?" said the lawyer. "You must ask a clergyman that."

"Oh, Mr. Underwood, I *wish* you were here!" cried Freda, wringing her hands. "I *wonder* if his soul is in heaven! I *can't* think it is—he was so *horrid!* What *could* his soul do in heaven? Oh dear! oh dear! I wish he hadn't died. I never thought for a moment he *could* die!"

"Did you ever think you could die yourself, young lady?" asked he dryly.

Again Freda raised her hands with a gesture in the air, as if to push him away.

"Oh, I couldn't die!" she cried beseechingly. "I am not fit—I am *not* fit. I can't think of dying—I am so young!"

Young she looked, young and distressed; and innocent and sweet enough to die that moment, and go straight up to heaven-land, if innocence and sweetness could purchase redemption.

"Well," said the lawyer, regarding her curiously as a specimen of human nature such as had not been brought under his notice before, "you and I must die, and *he* is dead."

Freda sat down. She really could not stand.

"It is very, very shocking !" she said after a pause. "I can't *think* how anything so shocking *could* happen !"

"Uncommonly shocking things *do* happen," said the lawyer dryly. "Now, Mrs. Vane, if you have become accustomed to this—to be accustomed is really all you require"—He paused, as if fearing to be too abrupt, and said rather apologetically, "You see I knew you were not happy together. I had to arrange the separation, you know, and——"

"Not *happy !*" cried Freda, almost wildly; "I was *miserable !* I could not have lived."

"You were miserable !" was the calm rejoinder—"and he ?"

"I never thought about *that*," replied she simply.

"Exactly ; you never thought about that. And in a marriage where one party avowedly only thinks of herself, there cannot, perhaps, be much happiness for the other."

" There was none for anybody," cried Freda ; " how could there be ?"

" Your marriage—*the* marriage, I mean—was a most unhappy and ill-assorted one," continued the lawyer. " You married on a fortnight's acquaintance or so ; you lived together three months ; you then, by mutual consent, separated, and have lived apart for six—and now he is dead. Such is the history of the marriage. It cannot be supposed, therefore, that you are more than startled and shocked by the communication I have made. There is not any *sorrow*—in the usual signification of the word."

" I am as sorry as ever I can be," cried she, with naïve sincerity.

" Well, you are sorry—of course, that is natural—but you will be able to attend to business, I hope ; for I am a busy man, Mrs. Fane, and have really very little time to spare."

" What business can there be ?" cried Freda impatiently ; " what more is there but *death?*" she started and shivered as she spoke the word. " Death !" she repeated ; "oh, it is horrible ! And afterwards ? Ah, there you cannot help me. You tell me to ask a clergyman ; but can a clergyman really tell where his soul is ? Can a clergyman guess ?"

" It is indecorous and uncharitable to express a doubt," said Mr. Crawford gravely. "Excuse me, Mrs. Fane, but such thoughts should not be expressed. It is very indecorous."

" Indecorous !" cried Freda with astonishment.

" I have Mr. Fane's will in my pocket," said the lawyer briskly.

" Have you ?" was the reply, spoken with languid indifference.

He eyed her sharply, and saw that the indifference was not assumed.

" What do you expect to do ? How and where will you live now ?" he asked.

" Oh," she said, " yes. I know what you mean. He paid the money for me here, and I wrote to you if I wanted anything. To be sure, that is all over now. I think I had better go to my uncle in Jamaica ; had not I ?

He was ill, and they thought it best for me to wait here, in case he had to come home on sick leave. But I don't think they can be coming home, and, at any rate, I might go out and see."

She spoke very much as if she was proposing to step out to the baker's in the next street, and see why the bread had not been sent.

"Well," replied he, "I have Mr. Fane's will in my pocket."

"I don't mind," she said; "he *can* have no power over me now"—she sighed as she said it. "I can do what I like, and go where I please; his will is powerless now," she added, with an unconscious pun.

"His will decides what is to be done with his property."

"His property?"

"Yes, his property and money. By the law, you are entitled to one-third of all he possessed, unless his will contains anything to the contrary;" and the lawyer slapped the pocket that contained the document as he spoke.

"To be sure, I have heard my aunt say

that of people," replied she; " how stupid of me not to think of it! I really did not under-stand what you meant."

Mr. Crawford produced the will.

" Perhaps you would like some witnesses while I read it ?"

" Witnesses while you read it! Read what? Why?" said she, all abroad. " Oh, you can't think how uncomfortable I feel! Couldn't you go away ?" then she got up and paced the room restlessly. " He is dead !" she cried; " he is dead! Lionel Fane is dead —my husband is dead !"

The lawyer opened the will; he began reading the preamble aloud, but Freda stopped him.

" It is nonsense !" she said indignantly; " don't; we ought to be reading prayers, if anything. Oh no, it is too late; prayers are not of any use now. I wish I was a Roman Catholic !" she cried, sudden light coming into her eyes; " that is the very thing—they pray for their souls. I wonder whether I could become a Roman Catholic! I know so little about what the differences really are, that I don't think it could signify; do you ?" and she turned eagerly to him, evidently wishing for his opinion.

"The girl is a fool!" thought Mr. Crawford, and he put the precious document back into his pocket. "I think, if you will allow me," he said aloud, "I will write to you. I will not trouble you now."

"But need you write?" she asked deprecatingly.

"Yes, I will write; there is a good deal to communicate, and it would be better to do it by letter."

"Yes, much better," she gladly assented; "and there is no occasion to be in a hurry about it. I don't the least mind waiting. I had *rather* wait. Shall I ring the bell, or can you let yourself out?"

She held out her hand to him, almost smiling. She did not in the least wish to be rude, but to be rid of him, to be alone, to be able to think, untormented by what she considered his useless chatter, was all she cared for. He had proposed to go, and she had every inclination to speed the parting guest.

Mr. Crawford almost laughed; the whole thing appeared to him indescribably ludicrous

—and perhaps it was so. He buttoned up the will, took her proffered hand, and made his bow.

" I will write to you, and communicate the contents of my client's will," he said.

And so they parted.

And on her eighteenth birthday Freda Fane found herself a widow.

CHAPTER V.

MONEY AND MONEY'S WORTH.

FOR the rest of that day Freda did
not know what to do with herself.
She felt as if she was in a dream
—a dream from which she could never wake.
To her it seemed as if the world had stood
still, and would not move on again—as if all
was changed—everything—everybody, and
this only because she was changed herself. She
could never, never, never be the same Freda;
her old self had gone out of her, and no new
self had come instead. The body was just to
live on, with a set of vague, inconceivable
thoughts struggling together within it, that
came to no conclusions, and never would or

could come to any conclusions whatsoever. These could not make a soul, and so she was a body without a soul.

She suddenly undressed herself, and went to bed by the dim twilight of a winter's evening; there she lay for hours, staring on the moonlight flickering against the wall, with wide-opened burning eyes. She was not thinking about anything; there was nothing within her, she knew, that could think.

Freda was gone—and no one else had come into her body instead. Then, in a moment, without anything to lead to it, her wide-opened burning eyes filled. with tears and in another moment they overflowed, and the tears streamed down her cheek one after another, as if they could never stop at all, and so they went on, and on, and on, till Freda had cried herself to sleep—for Freda was only eighteen years old.

In the morning she woke, feeling quite well and refreshed; she sprang from her bed.

"What is it? what is it?"

Then she remembered.

"Lionel Fane is dead! And his soul

is somewhere — where ? It *must* be in heaven. It would be too horrible to think of it if it were anywhere else. But what *could* it do in heaven ? And what an angel he would make—so dark !" Then she shuddered and wondered, if *she* should die, would her soul be fit for heaven either ? She ran to the glass and looked earnestly, eagerly, at the vision of beauty it reflected. " I shall make a *nice* angel," she cried, " while *he*—" and here she shuddered again ; " and if his soul *is* in heaven, and mine goes there too, shall we hate each other always ? But it does not matter if we do ; that is a *good* part of heaven—we shan't be married !"

Here the servant brought her a letter, for the post had just come in. She regarded it with displeased eyes.

" From that horrid lawyer," she said. " Well, I must read it, I suppose, but I need not answer it."

So she opened her letter, and read as follows :

" DEAR MADAM,
                    " It is my duty to inform you of

the position in which my late lamented client, Mr. Fane, left his affairs, and to forward you a copy of his will, which I herewith do. You will perceive by it, that at the period of his death he possessed private means to the amount of three thousand pounds a year; he has left five hundred pounds a year to his sister, Mrs. Fanshaw, who is with her husband, Major Fanshaw, in India, and one thousand pounds a year to you absolutely; the remaining fifteen hundred pounds is to be paid into the hands of trustees, and to accumulate till you are of age, when the interest of the accumulated sum will also become yours absolutely. The principal you will not be able to touch till you are thirty years of age, when the whole property becomes yours to do what you like with. The date is the 19th of May, being, I believe, the day *before* his marriage.

"I remain, madam,

"Your obedient servant,

"Joshua Crawford.

"P.S.—I enclose a letter and a paragraph from the paper giving an account of your husband's death."

The printed paragraph was out of a colonial newspaper, and ran as follows :

" We regret to have the painful duty of announcing the unexpectedly premature decease of a young and accomplished English gentleman, a visitor among us. One moment in the enjoyment of health, strength and life, the next launched into eternity. *Sic transit gloria mundi,* as the poet only too truly says. Mr. Lionel Fane was riding a horse full of vigour and spirit, which, notwithstanding the splendid qualities of the rider, contrived to get the bit between his teeth, and running away with him, hurled him to his fate, over the tremendous edge of a gravel-pit. The possessor of excellent abilities, which had shown themselves in a very gentlemanly profession and considerable private property, lay dead. There is *no* difference between the prince and the beggar. The funeral will take place to-morrow, in the most gratifying manner, and a large circle of relations in England will be placed in mourning by it ; but in this world submission is our only law, and the mysteries of Providence are inscrutable."

Freda's eyes skimmed over the paragraph, scarcely taking in the absurdities that veiled the fact. She then read the letter.

" Sir,

" I enclose a paragraph from the *Universal Informer*, narrating the melancholy accident that befell an English gentleman of the name of Fane. He survived it an hour, and requested me to write to you, with instructions that you will inform Mrs. Fane of the sad event, and take measures that his will is carried out in every respect. The accident occurred about a fortnight ago, in a wild part of the country, so that the medical advice which I summoned at once was not in time to be of any use. He suffered very little pain.

" Believe me, dear sir,

" Yours sincerely,

" F. Robinson."

Freda walked restlessly about the room after reading this.

" Why, it is a long time ago," she cried; "it is five weeks ago—it is all over—it is nothing new. He has been dead five weeks ;

he has been buried five weeks—it is not even new."

She did not know what she meant, or what she was feeling, but she kept repeating this as if she was a little out of her mind.

Then came a gentle tap at the door, and Mrs. Briggs entered : a small, thin woman, with sharp eyes and a sharp nose with a red tip to it; a dull, well-behaved person, whom nobody liked, and everybody respected—quite a pattern schoolmistress.

She came up to Freda, and kissed her.

" I condole with you in this dreadful afflic-tion," she said, with the greatest propriety ; "but it is the lot of human nature. These things are ordered by One who knows what is good for us better than we do ourselves, and we must not repine."

" 'Submission is our only law, and the mys-teries of Providence are inscrutable,'" said Freda, for the words were ringing in her head, and something in the turning of Mrs. Briggs' phrases made her reproduce them, almost without knowing that she did so.

" Indeed, yes," cried the schoolmistress, surprised and impressed ; " I am very glad to find you in this frame of mind—very glad indeed."

" It is all very sudden and shocking," said the girl. " I can't get accustomed to it; I don't know what to do, and it happened five weeks ago !"

" Time has a blessed influence," said Mrs. Briggs ; " time soothes sorrow."

" I am not unhappy, you know," replied Freda frankly; "but I am shocked, and I don't want to pretend anything—but I don't know what to do."

" Tears will bring relief," began Mrs. Briggs ; but Freda interrupted her.

" I cried dreadfully last night," she said ; " and it's horrid. I don't want to cry any more ; it makes my eyes very uncomfortable."

" You have cried, and you are resigned," said Mrs. Briggs ; " you do not repine ; there is nothing more to be wished. You will gradually relax your—your—you will, I mean, come among us again in time ; and you will read your Bible. I do not see how anything can be better, under the very trying circumstances that must always attend a death."

"I shall go to Jamaica," replied Freda simply.

"Oh, I hope not!" cried Mrs. Briggs, startled out of her propriety. Freda paid well.

"I want to go up to London, and then to Jamaica."

"Yes—well—you can do both in time; but I hope there is no hurry."

"That is the worst of it," said she; "I feel so hurried—I don't like keeping still—I want to be doing something. I have a hurry all through me—I wonder why," she added, with a helpless look, "for there is none really. I think if I went out and ran hard it would go off."

Mrs. Briggs was naturally enough, scandalised at the idea of the newly-made widow going out and running hard; but she only said :

"A few drops of red lavender on a lump of sugar is *very* efficacious, in times of trouble."

Freda walked up and down the room very fast, and muttered to herself, "Red fiddlesticks."

"Will you permit me to order the necessary things for you," continued Mrs. Briggs—"to take that sad but inevitable work off your hands?" And she sighed, as it was right she should, when referring to mourning.

"I don't want anything, thank you," was the apparently strange reply.

"Oh, my dear Mrs. Fane, you must have bombazine and crape up to here," marking her own figure near the waist, "and caps, and a crape bonnet and veil. You must have everything new—everything."

"I thought you meant lavender on sugar," cried Freda; "why, I must have mourning—I never thought of that; and caps! how extraordinary! Why, I am a widow!" And she stopped short, and stared Mrs. Briggs in the face with a look of the most utter astonishment, as if this view of the case had only just burst on her and overwhelmed her, as it did so. "I am a widow!"

"Poor dear!" said that lady soothingly; "so young too—it is very touching—very."

"Oh!" cried Freda, "may Corabel come to me. I *like* Corabel—do let her come.

I am frightened." And she began to cry again.

"I will send Miss Bell to you with pleasure," said the schoolmistress firmly; "she is engaged now, instructing the second class in English history, but I will allow her to postpone the lessons in consideration of your sad position. Miss Bell shall attend you immediately; and in the meantime, my dear Mrs. Fane, will you permit me to send the necessary orders to a dressmaker and milliner, so that there may be no delay, except that which cannot be avoided, in procuring your mourning? Your mind naturally shrinks from such sad details at present, and I would be glad to save you as much as I can."

"Thanks—yes, please do. I shouldn't have a notion what to order. Oh, how very, very odd it is! How I do wish Mr. Underwood was at home!"

Mr. Underwood, Mrs. Briggs felt, could hardly be as efficient in choosing the crape garments as she should; but she was much too proper not to consider that clergymen had their own place in times of affliction, and that Mrs. Fane's wish to see one was quite correct. She went away fairly satisfied with her interview, and sent Miss Bell to the sufferer.

Cora Bell, or Corabel, as Freda called her, was the English teacher, and Freda's principal friend in the establishment, where all were none the less her friends, for our heroine was a universal favourite at school. Miss Bell was a great contrast to Freda, and perhaps on that very account her principal friend. She was about two-and-twenty, of middle height and nice figure; fair and pale, with kind grey eyes, and a face that was not actually pretty, though its expression was sweet and modest.

She was what is generally called an interesting girl. People who looked at her once might not look at her twice, but if they did they were pretty sure to look at her a third time also. She had good manners, and seldom spoke thoughtlessly or impulsively, and she was very kind and unselfish; a vein of melancholy ran through her character when well known, but her exterior was always calm and cheerful. She and Freda first made friends over their studies, and they had grown intimate in many a long talk during leisure-hours, and liked each other sincerely, though neither had spoken much to the other of herself, her family, or her position.

Miss Bell would not have thought of intruding on the young widow unsummoned; but hastened to her the minute she found she had expressed a wish to see her. She entered a little timidly, with a doubtful questioning face, and going straight up to her, put her arm round her, and silently kissed her.

"They all kiss me," thought Freda; but she liked it, and felt as if the hurry within her was subsiding.

She was the first to speak.

"You have heard?" she said. "Is not it shocking?"

"My poor Freda!" replied Corabel, "it is dreadful—I can't comfort you."

"I don't want comfort. I am not unhappy —but it is so *shocking*. I can't *help* feeling it, you know, Corabel, though I am *not* unhappy."

"And I can't help being glad you are not unhappy—at least, that it is not a great

affliction, to make you quite miserable for
ever, as it might have been."

Freda shook her head. " It is not a great
affliction," she said, " but it is very shocking !
and I don't seem to understand it. Oh !
Corabel, shall I get accustomed to it, and
not mind it ? I *wish* I didn't mind it.
I *never* got accustomed to being married—
not in the whole three months—and so I ran
away, and there was an end of it; but I *can't*
run away from *this.* And what shall I do
if I don't get accustomed to it ?"

She looked with pitiful, childlike eyes into
Cora's, which filled with tears as she answered
her soothingly :

" You *will* get accustomed to it ; one does
to everything, otherwise nobody could go on
living."

" It is all such a mistake," sighed Freda ;
" I *meant* life to be so happy, and first one
thing comes and then another, to spoil it. I
was really happy here, and now I don't know
what to do !"

" That feeling will go off. You will gradually be as usual."

" I am a widow !" cried Freda. " It seems

27—2

impossible, but I am. I am to have crape up
to here," touching herself as Mrs. Briggs had
done ; " and caps. I am a widow, Corabel !
It seems impossible, but I am."

" Dear Freda, don't mind all those sort of
feelings ; you will get accustomed to all that
very soon."

" It is a whole day since, with a night in
the middle of it," said Freda, " and it seems
like months and months, and yet I am not
one bit accustomed."

" Think what it would have been if you
had loved him."

" I couldn't have loved him. I don't understand girls loving men. Do you think
they ever do, really ? I *can't* understand it."

" Yes, I think they do really, sometimes,"
replied Miss Bell very quietly.

" I want to go to my uncle and aunt in
Jamaica."

" How I shall miss you !" said Miss Bell.

" You shall go with me. Yes ; why not ?
Do I" And the old Freda had come back
again in the eager, childlike, sweet imperious-
ness with which she spoke.

" I ? Oh, that is impossible."

" Not a bit of it. I have heaps and heaps
of money—a thousand a year, or something
or other, already, and lots when I am of age ;
and anything you can think of, I'm not quite
sure what, when I am thirty—as if it mattered *what* one has when one is as old as *that*
—and I will take you to Jamaica with me, if
you will only be good and come."

Miss Bell smiled, and a bright colour rose
into her cheeks.

" It is very kind of you to wish it. I am
very fond of you," she said. " You could not
go alone, and I *might*, perhaps, accompany
you as your companion ; but it is all too
sudden to think of settling anything ; you
must speak to that lawyer, and see what your
friends say."

" Indeed, no," cried Freda, and she was a
queen again now ; " that lawyer has nothing
to do with me, and I have no friends. I
shall do exactly what I like. I shall go to
Jamaica, and I shall take you with me. I think
it will be good fun——" Here she stopped
short. " I don't suppose I mean *that*, do I ?"
said she slowly. " Oh, Corabel, I am getting
accustomed to it already !"

"Yes, there is nothing to prevent you, Freda. It is not a great sorrow. It is a shock and a wound, but you will soon get over that."

"I really believe I shall," said Freda, surprised; "and I thought I never should. How very odd!"

Two or three days afterwards Freda told Mrs. Briggs she was going to London for the evening, by train, and might she take Miss Bell with her?

Mrs. Briggs demurred at Freda's making an excursion, and before her mourning had come home, but finally consented, as she reflected that she knew no one she was likely to meet there, and graciously gave Miss Bell leave to accompany her.

So to London Freda and her friend went. She desired the cabman whom they secured at the station to drive slowly along the streets with the best shops, and stop when she told him; and she made him pull up at the door of a great upholsterer's.

There the two girls got out, and Freda went all over the establishment, looking for chairs and tables. She chose a work-table

and a writing-table and two easy-chairs, and
one was to be a gentleman's and the other a
lady's, and she ordered to have names
" stamped, or embroidered, or anything," on
the back of each chair ; on the gentleman's
chair the name was to be " Jack," and on the
lady's chair it was to be " Letty."

" It is very pleasant having money," she
remarked, " and it is nice beyond everything
spending it on others.   People who can make
presents never can be *very* unhappy."   Then
she turned suddenly to the shopman, and
said : " Oh, will you tell me where I can buy
pigs."

" Buy pigs ?" repeated the shopman, with a
vague look.

" Yes," she replied calmly ; and then reiterated, with rather a raised voice, as if she
thought he was a little deaf, " pigs."

" Pigs ?" answered he helplessly, " what
sort of pigs ?"

It was hardly a relevant question, but it
may be supposed that he thought he *must*
have misunderstood her.

" Any sort," she answered readily ; " but
where can I buy them ?"

"Do you mean—pigs?" said he slowly; "animals?"

"Of course I do. What's the matter? Where can I buy pigs?"

"Oh, you can't get them in London," said the man, looking earnestly at her, and then turning an appealing glance to her companion, as much as to ask, "Is she mad?"

"Not get them in London!" cried Freda, with indignant unbelief; "why, you can buy everything in London."

"Not pigs," said the man glibly.

"You can buy everything in London except pigs!" exclaimed she, astonished. "How *very* odd. Don't you *think* I could get them somewhere? Is not there Smithfield? Couldn't I get them there? Where is it?"

"Well, no," said the shopman, examining her face still more earnestly, "I don't think you could."

"How stupid!" cried Freda. "Well, I really *am* disappointed."

When they had left the shop, Corabel asked rather anxiously:

"What *can* you want with pigs, my dear Freda?"

" Why, for Jack, to be sure," cried Freda, still indignant and unbelieving. " Jack *dotes* upon pigs. I'm sure it's not true that they can't be bought in London."

Then Freda went into a jeweller's shop and purchased a twenty-guinea diamond pin, and a five-guinea opal ring, and a five-guinea locket, and a ten-guinea chain. She put the locket on the chain, and, cutting a bit of hair from her own head, desired that it might be placed in it; this done, she threw the chain over Miss Bell's neck, saying:

" There ! The pin is for my dear friend, and the ring for his sister," she cried gaily. " Oh, how nice it is !"

Freda had only a few pounds in her pocket, and the jeweller demurred when she proposed to take the things away with her without paying for them. He asked for a reference, which she considered a horribly mean thing to do. However, she said he might send the parcel and the bill to Mr. Crawford, Queen Anne's Street ; only it must be done at once, and she would drive there and have the things paid for.

" He has got all my money," she remarked

calmly, " and so he will pay for whatever I buy. But I must drive there at once, and you must send my parcels there at once, or I shall not get back to school in time."

Like other children, she appeared to take it for granted that everybody knew who she was, and all about her. And after buying this expensive jewellery, she was not in the least troubled by any idea of the oddity of talking of going " back to school."

But the jeweller thought it extremely odd, to say the least of it ; and making up the packet of pretty gems, himself took them to No. —, Queen Anne's Street, following the ladies' cab in another.

Freda burst into Mr. Crawford's office like a sunbeam, Miss Bell calmly following her.

" Here's a man coming with things I've bought, and here are the bills for you to pay, please," cried the client, flinging down the little bits of paper before him.

Mr. Crawford gravely perused them, with their items of rings, pins, lockets, and chains.

" Your income will not allow of your spending forty or fifty pounds on trinkets,

Mrs. Fane," he said civilly ; "and, in deep mourning, you can't wear them."

Freda flashed her eyes upon him.

" Thank you," she replied, with equal civility, " I will spend my income as I like, and the trumpery is not for myself. It's for my friends," she added loftily.

" Well, that may be ; but it makes no difference. Two hundred and fifty pounds I am to pay into your bankers—they are to last you three months. You must pay Miss Briggs out of them, and you must pay out of them for everything you want. This is a pretty large hole to make in such a sum already."

" These things *had* to be bought," replied she coolly. " They are necessaries. No one does without necessaries, except in the workhouse." ·

" Oh, is that your view ?"

" No, it is not my view, it is the fact ; so please pay this stupid old man as soon as he comes, Mr. Crawford, and don't say anything more about it."

" I will pay him, certainly. But I hope I shall have no more such bills to pay."

" You will have another for chairs and

tables. Let me see, how much was it, Corabel? Jack's chair was seven pounds and his table fifteen, and her table was three pounds ten and her chair five pounds five, wasn't it? That's—oh, my dear Corabel, how much *is* that?"

" Are you going to take a house and furnish it, Mrs. Fane?"

" No, I am not, Mr. Crawford. These are for friends."

" Well, that is thirty or forty pounds more, I suppose. You have spent eighty or ninety pounds already. I shall have very little more than one hundred and fifty to pay in to your bankers for you. Pray excuse me if I advise you to be a little careful, and not to spend your money quite so fast, or you will get yourself into difficulties which it will be quite out of my power to rescue you from."

" You?" cried Freda, unaffectedly astonished ; " why I should never *think* of asking you to help me. You are a lawyer!"

The jeweller now making his appearance, Mr. Crawford paid him on the delivery of the goods, and handed the receipted bills to Freda.

" What's this for ?" she asked.

"To keep."

"Oh, I don't want them. Why did you make him write ' paid ' here ? I think it's rather mean ; as if we did not all of us know that it *is* paid. Where's the use ?"

Mr. Crawford stared and said nothing : and the jeweller remarked blandly that it was always better to do business in a regular manner.

Then Freda turned her back on the lawyer, and opened the cases, and looked caressingly at the pretty, shining creatures within them, making an evident, secret fuss, pretending that no one was to see. She glanced slily over her shoulder.

" Wouldn't you like a peep ?" she said, in a tantalising manner. And, as Mr. Crawford did not reply, she turned suddenly and flashed them close under his eyes for an instant, then ran away, shutting them up, and crying out, " Don't you really care for pretty things ? Oh, you must !—everybody must. Wouldn't you like some one to give *you* a diamond pin ?" And she burst into a sweet, childlike laugh, at the idea. " Come, Corabel," she cried,

" we shall be late. It is best for us to get back to school as quickly as we can, or we shan't find any supper." Then she made a graceful curtsey, and said very politely and sweetly to Mr. Crawford : " Good evening. I am *so* much obliged to you."

And the sunshine left the room with her as she went home.

CHAPTER VI.

OLD FRIENDS AND NEW.

MR. AND MISS UNDERWOOD had been abroad for many months. The complete change was ordered as actually necessary for Maud's health, and her brother, rendered very anxious by the opinion of the doctors, engaged a curate for six months, and left him in charge of his living. For some time the move seemed only a doubtful good. The invalid's spirits were so low that that alone, rendered her hold on life insecure and feeble. Oh, the blessing of elastic spirits! a blessing known to Freda, and unknown to Maud. The happy ones who possess the gift—and it is a gift almost as much as either beauty or genius—should, in truth, be very gentle and considerate to those, the unhappy, who have it not. Of the earth, earthy, are the spirits that sink into depression.

"Hark, the lark at heaven's gate sings."

But though of the earth, earthy, such spirits may be as fine and sensitive (many even more so), as those that rise. It is earth *keeping down* what was *meant* for heaven, and *therefore* they are depressed; while, in the other case, the happy ones sing at heaven's gate, undepressed by earth.

Poor Maud, sunk deeply in languor and depression, seemed powerless to rise from the dreary abyss, and was slipping out of life from mere want of will to remain in it. Her brother watched and nursed her with the tenderness of a woman and the strength of a man, and France and Italy did all they could to help him, which was very little indeed. But Switzerland did more. Who can resist Switzerland? To the well and the young, Switzerland is rapture; to the sick and the sorry it is comfort, and comfort of that exquisite kind that makes the need for

comfort forgotten.   Oh, snow-covered moun-
tains, emerald valleys, and lovely lakes, take
unto yourselves the happy allegiance of
all hearts—the tender gratitude of many.
Switzerland ! the very name is enough.   Yes,
I, too, have been in Arcadia.

The colour stole back into Maud's cheeks ;
the light into her eyes ; and the wish to live
into her heart.   Could they help doing so ?
She was in Switzerland.

To see his sister recovering was enough for
Lewes Underwood, and in the unselfish life
he led, he found the best balm for his own
wounds.   Besides, was not he too in Switzerland ?

But all things must come to an end.
Should we value them so much if they did
not ? Sages say, No ; but I say, Yes we
should, and a thousand times more.   Endless
youth, love, and joy ! Shall we *not* value
them ?   Is heaven then a dream ?

The time came when Maud was well enough
to return to England, and then home duties
called with imperative voice, on Lewes to
neglect them no longer.

It is very delightful to go abroad, and

it is extremely pleasant to come home
again.

" ' England, with all thy faults I love thee still ! ' "

cried Lewes Underwood, laughing, as the
white cliffs of Dover came in sight.

> " ' I like the taxes, when they're not too many ;
>   I like a sea-coal fire, when not too dear ;
> I like a beefsteak, too, as well as any,
>   Have no objection to a pot of beer ;
> I like the weather when it is not rainy —
>   That is, I like two months in every year.'

So said Lord Byron, and so has many an
Englishman felt, since Lord Byron lay in his
Grecian grave."

" Yes," replied Maud absently, "of course ;
only we do have very fine days."

" Even in England—and here we are, to
enjoy one of them," cried Lewes joyously,
as he was one of the first of the passengers
who sprang on shore.

The brother and sister drove together to a
quiet hotel in Jermyn Street, where they
ordered dinner, and Maud lay down to
rest.

Lewes Underwood found himself with a

few hours at his own disposal between the present moment, and that appointed for dinner. He had only one idea of what to do with this time—there was not a single doubt in his mind about that. He put himself into a train, and went down to Clapham, and when there, to Mrs. Briggs' Seminary for Young Ladies, where, ringing at the hall-door, he inquired if Mrs. Fane was at home.

The servant stared at him with some astonishment, and replied in the negative.

He felt very unreasonably surprised and disappointed, but recovering himself asked for Mrs. Briggs, and was at once shown into that lady's private sitting-room. He was kept waiting the orthodox ten minutes, during which it may be supposed that Mrs. Briggs was changing her cap and putting on her cameo-brooch, and giving any other slight necessary adornments to her person. After which she entered the room, with the proud and pleasant consciousness on her mind that in all ways Mrs. Briggs was—what Mrs. Briggs should be.

It was a little disappointment to her to find her visitor a young man. Too young for it to be possible for him to put his children (if he had children) to any school, except one that goes by the name of an Infant School: but she cheered up as she thought, " Sisters, if not daughters ;" and she cheered up still more when she perceived that he was a clergyman, and might therefore be a recommender and referee for any other men's daughters or sisters. If the liberty to wear a white tie in the morning carries some inconveniences along with it, it brings many privileges also, and none more than the feeling of universal confidence that little bit of white muslin inspires.

Mrs. Briggs relaxed her thin features into a smile that beamed with propriety, crossed her hands over her waist, and made her most elegant slight bend and slighter curtsey.

" I beg pardon for troubling you," said her visitor a little abruptly, " but I called to see Mrs. Fane."

No new pupils then. Mrs. Briggs' appearrance changed a good deal, the natural vinegar replacing the assumed oil.

" Ah, poor young woman !" she said.

" Good heavens!" cried the clergyman, with a great start, " is anything the matter with her ?"

Mrs. Briggs shook her head with a most correct amount of mournfulness.

" She has left me, sir.   She is gone——"

Mr. Underwood drew a deep breath.   He had felt almost paralysed by a nameless terror.   The relief was great.

" She has rejoined her husband, perhaps ?" he asked with anxiety.

" No, sir, she has not rejoined her husband —for a sufficient reason—doubtless she will at the appointed time ; but for the present he is in heaven, and she is in Jamaica."

" Heaven and Jamaica !" repeated the bewildered priest.

" You have not then, perhaps, heard that Mr. Fane is dead ?" said Mrs. Briggs, with that natural pleasure everybody takes in communicating a shocking piece of news.

Mr. Underwood stared her in the face, and frightened her by actually becoming quite white.   He seemed more overcome by the news of the man's death than his own wife had been.

"Lionel Fane dead!" he cried at last. "Oh no, no! Don't say so."

"We must all die," replied the school-mistress in her element, and thoroughly at home in it. "We must all die, and we must all mourn for those who are taken, in this vale of tears—and we must submit to the decrees of Providence. I hope, sir, you will allow me to offer you a glass of wine and a biscuit. You are naturally overcome."

"Lionel Fane dead!" he repeated. "Poor fellow! Oh, poor fellow! Where and when?" added he, with an abrupt questioning, Mrs. Briggs felt was quite out of place.

She answered him slowly, and with a good many words, to atone for his indecent brevity.

"It was the will of Providence to remove him from this earthly scene to a better world, about six months ago, in Australia. Our loss is his gain, and it would be selfishness to wish him back. He was thrown from his horse, and died shortly afterwards. The notices in the papers were most gratifying. The funeral was everything those nearest to him could desire, and his lawyer communicated the news of the sad event to his widow, in the most correct and proper manner. She is left exceedingly well off. The will was quite what it should be. It was a very anxious time for those who were with the chief mourner, but, listening to words of consolation, she soon shed tears, and declared herself to be resigned. We have a great deal to be thankful for." And Mrs. Briggs cast up her eyes, and then cast them down, just exactly as eyes should be first cast up and then cast down, under the circumstances.

"My poor Lionel!" was all the reply. "And is Freda in Jamaica?"

"Mrs. Lionel Fane *is* in Jamaica," answered the schoolmistress in a tone of mild reproof.

Lewes Underwood remained a moment or two lost in thought, his eyes fixed on the floor, his hands thrust deep into his pockets. Then he looked suddenly up like a man waking from a dream, with a sorrowful worn look in his eyes, as if he had suffered for days instead of minutes.

"Will you kindly give me the lawyer's name and address?" said he.

Mrs. Briggs politely complied, and he wrote it down at her dictation. He then apologised for his visit, thanked her, and went hastily away.

"And that is a clergyman!" said she in pious horror, as the door closed behind his retreating form; "a clergyman of the ESTAB-LISHED CHURCH!"

Mr. Underwood was not at all aware of the indignation he had excited, or of how very improper his conduct was considered to be, and if he had been, I am afraid he would not have cared much about it. He went straight from Mrs. Briggs', Clapham Common, to Mr. Crawford, Queen Anne Street, Westminster, and learned from him all that there was to learn about Freda. Mr. Crawford communicated the particulars of Mr. Fane's death, and of his will, and of the departure of his widow for Jamaica.

"And a most unaccountable young woman his widow is," said Mr. Crawford with emphasis, and peering at Mr. Underwood from under his spectacles—"most unaccountable."

"She is very young," replied the clergyman deprecatingly.

"Old enough to be married," said the lawyer sharply.

"She is younger than her years," urged the other.

"Begging your pardon, Mr. Underwood, that is a sort of thing I never understand or see the sense of. What business have people to be younger than their years? If a man of fifty behaves like a foolish boy of twenty-five, I can't see that it is any excuse for him to say that he is younger than his age. On the contrary, that is just what we are blaming him for, isn't it?"

"Freda is not fifty," replied Lewes, with something almost like a smile twitching at the corners of his mouth, as the idea of fifty years of age, and Freda, came into his mind in conjunction. The thought seemed to strike the lawyer as forcibly, though in a different way. He threw up his hands and eyes.

"No, she is not fifty. My conscience, Mr. Underwood, what a woman of fifty she will make!"

"And she has really sailed for Jamaica?" sighed the clergyman. "She is really there now? Who accompanied her, Mr. Crawford? How was it all managed?"

" A very nice, proper, well-behaved young lady went with her as companion," said Mr. Crawford. " I only hope it will not be a disadvantage to her, and that Mrs. Fane will not get into scrapes, and drag this girl into the mire along with her. I took their passages for them and saw them off, and manage her money. She did not write on her arrival, but her uncle, Major Cameron, did, and indeed I had much rather arrange the business matters through him, than with the lady herself. She is a very objectionable client, Mr. Underwood ·—a very objectionable client indeed."

Here the lawyer looked for sympathy to the clergyman, who, however, did not give him any, by word or by sign.

" She was not in the least cut up by her husband's death—not in the least. I never saw such an unfeeling girl in my life."

" It was a very unhappy marriage."

" Yes, it was a very unhappy marriage; and whose fault was that, pray? I think poor Fane was your intimate friend, Mr. Underwood?"

" He was," replied he with much emotion.
" He was the most intimate and dearest friend
I ever had."

" The girl made him miserable, broke his
heart, wrecked his life, and didn't care two-
pence for his death."

" Perhaps she cared more than she showed,"
replied Lewes with a good deal of hesitation.
" It is very difficult to judge of how much
or how little, people feel ; they don't always
know themselves, and I think it very
likely——"

Here he paused as the lawyer interrupted
him.

" She didn't care about the will either ; she
never asked a question ; it was nothing to her
whether she was a millionnaire or a beggar.
To tell you the truth, Mr. Underwood, I
believe she's a fool."

A little flush rose in Lewes's face, but it
was more like an expression of satisfaction
than of anger.

" She is perfectly disinterested," he said in
a low voice.

The lawyer looked sharply at him.

" That's not possible," he said with deci-

sion, " unless you are a fool. No sane person
can be or ought to be disinterested. You
must care about what you have and what
you haven't, and you'll end your days in the
workhouse if you don't. But I'll tell you
what, Mr. Underwood ; the young lady we
are speaking of knows how to spend money
if she doesn't care about *having* it. My goodness, didn't she make the notes fly—buying
presents right and left, furniture and jewels,
and everything you can think of, for farmers
and those sort of people !"

" Oh yes, I know ; very old friends to
whom she would wish to show kindness.
Really, Mr. Crawford, I don't see why Mrs.
Fane shouldn't spend her own money as she
likes."

" It will all be very well if she doesn't
spend it two or three times over, before she's
done. Mark my words, Mr. Underwood—if
ever a woman made herself notorious in this
world, that's a woman who will know how to
do it !"

" She is with her uncle and aunt now, and
this young lady friend, whom you say is all
that she should be, and probably she will

grow quiet and understand things as she gets older." (Oh, Mr. Underwood, are you saying what you really think? Freda quiet and understanding things!) "And in the meantime, Mr. Crawford, I must tell you that I really don't believe you do her justice —you have only seen one side of her character. She was in my house in a time of sickness and trouble, and no one could have behaved more kindly or thought less of herself, and more of other people."

" Oh, indeed!" said the lawyer dryly, " I really should not have expected it. But I'll tell *you* one thing, Mr. Underwood—she's an uncommonly pretty girl, and that goes an uncommonly long way with some people."

Lewes Underwood felt the colour, that he would fain have kept down, rise, and spread all over his face. But his manner remained calm and unembarrassed, as he rose and wished Mr. Crawford good-bye, thanking him for the information he had given him, and noting down Freda's address in Jamaica before he did so.

When he found himself out in the street again, he took off his hat for a minute, and felt refreshed by the breeze that blew about his head and face. Then he walked very slowly back to the hotel in Jermyn Street, with the grievous task before him, of telling his sister of their friend's death. It seemed as if he was always to have something to break to her about that poor friend—her early love—always something to tell her that must distress her, and might make her ill. Always? there never could be anything more to tell her after this, nothing more that could cause distress or pain, or produce illness— nothing more; it was all over, he was dead— dead! Lionel Fane was dead. And so he walked wearily on, thinking far more of the dead Lionel than of the living Freda. Freda was well and happy; yes, his heart told him she was happy because Lionel was dead. Freda was young, and her whole life stretched out before her to live. What was there to think of? Why should any one think about Freda? She was alive. And it was the dead—only the dead who were worthy of a thought. And Lionel was dead — Lionel Fane was dead!

Alas! why had not they parted better

friends ? They had not quarrelled certainly, but there had been misunderstandings, and an estrangement. Bitter words had been spoken by Lionel, and not retracted ; and he knew that Lewes had asked his wife to marry him after an acquaintance of three days. Oh, what a fool he had been, and why had he been such a fool ? Why had his folly obliged him to play so poor a part in those last interviews with his friend ? Was it true, as that particularly disagreeable lawyer had said, that a pretty face goes such an uncommonly long way with some people ? Had it really gone such a long way with him ? His acquaintance with, and love for Freda, seemed, now that he looked back on it through time and sorrow, to have been merely a dream—a beautiful, impossible dream ; the only *reality* was that Lionel Fane was dead !

Then he wondered a little about Freda, but only in connection with the dead Lionel, not as herself at all—only as his widow. What had she felt ? Who had told her ? Had his dearest Lionel's death, actually made her happy ? Had she in very truth hated him ? Did those radiant eyes of hers not shed one

tear for this man—this husband who had
loved her so passionately, whose heart she
had broken, whose life she had wrecked,
whose death she had caused? Here the
Vicar came to a standstill in the middle of
Regent Street, and took off his hat again,
that his fevered confused head might once
more woo the breeze of heaven which was
blowing even in Regent Street. A policeman stopped, looked at him, and asked
gently and respectfully if he was ill, and if
he could do anything for him. Lewes stared
at the man as if he did not understand anything, and then with the old water-dog shake,
which Freda would have known so well, came
back to himself.

His inclination would have been, whilst
staring at the policeman, to say out loudly
either the words " Lionel Fane is dead," or
" Freda is a widow." But he resisted the
inclination, as we all do resist those insane
impulses which I suppose most of us have
felt—is it the only difference between us and
the *mad*, that *we* overcome those impulses,
while the impulses overcome *them ?*—and
civilly thanking him, said that he had heard

some sudden bad news, and had been a little
upset by it. The policeman recommended
a cab, but Lewes informed him he was only
going into Jermyn Street, and touching their
hats to each other, each passed on his respective way.

"Would that we were out of London!
would that we were at home again! would
that Maud knew—or never need know! Why
should she ever know? He was in Australia—" here he stopped his thoughts, shud-
dering with a sort of fear. Yes, he *was* in
Australia—he need not have stopped himself
—dead and buried there; but even if he
was living there they might for months or
years hear nothing of him, and his name
need never be mentioned at all between
them. And Freda was in Jamaica; the
same might be said of her—her widowhood
might remain a thing unknown to Maud.
Why then should he unnecessarily give her
such a great grief, and perhaps—who could
tell?—inflict a serious illness upon her? At
all events he would be in no hurry—there
was no occasion for hurry; there need, alas!
never again be any hurry or haste about any-

thing that concerned Lionel Fane. So he
certainly would not tell her that evening, not
while they were in London; he would wait
till they had returned home, and then he
would try to gradually prepare her mind for
the calamity, and not let her know the dreadful fact till after days of preparation, so that
at any rate it should not come upon her all
at once, suddenly, as it had on him. Was it
really only two or three hours ago since he
had heard it—since Mrs. Briggs came into
her sitting-room and told him. And was it
really Mrs. Briggs who told him—and really
only two or three hours ago? It seemed as
if he had known it for years, and that the
knowledge had sprang up unassisted in his
own mind.

He was greatly surprised on entering this
little drawing-room in the hotel to find Maud
sitting up, to hear her speaking with great
animation, and to see that there was a gentleman with her. She turned to him eagerly
with sparkling eyes, and such a pretty pink
colour in her usually pale cheeks.

"Oh, Lewes, I am so glad you are come!"
she cried. "Do you know who this is?"

Another of those dreadful insane thoughts came across Lewes's mind (and again I wonder, is it merely the not yielding to such, instead of the yielding to them, that separates us from our mad brethren?) ; he turned with a sort of impossible expectation that he should see it was Lionel Fane who sat on the chair beside his sister—Lionel Fane whom he knew was lying dead in his Australian grave—and he almost started when, instead of him, he beheld a rather short, slight, fair, thoughtful-looking man, whose face was not quite unfamiliar to him, though he could not write any name to it.

" No," he said, rather vaguely, " I don't know who it is—ought I ?"

" I should have known you anywhere," said the stranger. " Yes—you ought—and you ought not ; it is years since you saw me, but you knew me very well once, I am——"

" Arthur Hilton," interrupted Mr. Underwood. " Oh, I know you very well now you speak, and that I have had time to look at you ; and I am uncommonly glad to see you.

29—2

Where in the world do you spring from, and how did you find us out ?"

" I met Miss Underwood on the stairs," replied Arthur Hilton quietly, " and recognised her immediately."

" But that *is* so strange," cried Maud, blushing and pleased, " for I am so very, very much changed since you saw me ; I was only a girl, and now I am almost an old woman, and a sickly one too."

Both the gentlemen laughed at this, for in these days eight-and-twenty is not considered almost an old woman ; and Maud Underwood at that moment, with her soft sparkling eyes and pink cheeks, looked quite young and quite pretty.

" I think you are very little changed ; as you came out of the door of your room, and as I ran up the stairs and met you face to face, I knew you that minute ; but you did not know me, Miss Underwood."

" No, I did not know you ; but I am a bad hand at remembering faces, and," she added eagerly, " Lewes did ; he knew you as soon as ever you spoke."

Mr. Hilton made no answer to that, and looked as if he somehow did not consider it quite the same thing.

"And what have you been doing all these years, Hilton?" said his friend. "And how is it we have never met you before, since we meet you now?"

"I am a doctor," he replied, "as you know I always meant to be ; but I had to doctor myself very soon. I got a touch on the lungs, and ordered myself out of England for a while. I have been practising in Rome all these years, and became the fashion, and made money as fast as a man need make it. And now I have been in London a few months, and have got into a very satisfactory practice here already."

"You are a lucky man, Hilton."

"I don't know about that. A man may be lucky in some things, without being a lucky man."

"You are married, of course?" said Maud, with a friendly curiosity.

"No, I am not married," replied Dr. Hilton, looking at her rather earnestly ; "but why of course, Miss Underwood?"

"Oh, because doctors always *have* to marry. I thought they could hardly be successful without wives."

" I am *not* married," reiterated Dr. Hilton; " but I should like to be."

At which candid confession the brother and sister both laughed.

CHAPTER VII.

DOCTOR HILTON.

AFTER he had laughed, Lewes Underwood felt a horrible dislike to himself for having done so. Was it possible that the sound that had just rung in his ears was the sound of his own laughter within a few hours of the moment when he had been told that Lionel Fane was dead? Was he really so heartless and so shallow? Then he began to wonder whether he *had* any heart or any feeling at all. *Did* he care for anybody? Oh yes, he loved people, of course, or had always believed that he did, and that life to him was chiefly what loving these people made it. And yet his dearest friend—his young, strong, healthy, powerful, *lifeful* friend—was dead—suddenly dead—killed in a minute by a fall from his horse; and he had just heard of it, and here he was sitting chatting—*chatting* with another friend, and laughing, actually laughing. Was it he who was heartless and mindless, or was life and love, and earth and heaven, only a farce and a delusion?

"I don't see anything to laugh at in a man wishing to be married," he found, when his attention came back to the conversation, that his friend was saying. "All young ladies are supposed to wish it—begging your pardon, Miss Underwood, for the liberty I am taking in saying so—and if young ladies, why not young men? It can't be supposed that the kind creatures wish to marry us against our wills, can it?"

"But you are assuming the question that young ladies do wish it," replied Maud gaily —with a gaiety that surprised Lewes, as it was unusual to her, and which grated on him in his present mood.

He felt a sort of anger as the idea *would* present itself to his mind that this very Maud, who now spoke so gaily, had wished to marry Lionel against his will, or, at least, had wished to marry him when he had not wished to marry her. "I dare say she will not care for his death," he thought perversely. "She will be like me, she will not care for it. Poor fellow! poor Lionel! does anybody care for your death, I wonder? Freda, I suppose, is glad—glad. And is anybody sorry? Who should mourn, if not your widow, and the woman who wished to be your wife, and your own familiar friend?"

Then he found that Dr. Hilton was going on talking.

"You see," he was saying, "I have a nice house—I think I may call it a very nice house—in Harley Street, which is undeniably one of the healthiest streets in London. My drawing-room is an uncommonly pretty room —it is indeed. I should like to show you my drawing-room. I shall have great pleasure in showing you my drawing-room. And I have a nice little brougham—C springs—Colling's patent axle. And a capital cob; no bearing-reins; but knows how to hold up his head, and step as he ought to do. And I have business and I have leisure; and I have quite as much money as I care to have, which is not what everybody can say—no, not what some fellows would say who are richer than I am. Really, Miss Underwood, I think you must admit that, not having a wife, I want one, and that I ought to have one."

"But with all this, and feeling so keenly the pleasure of having it all, *and* the want of the one thing you haven't got, I wonder very much why you haven't got it," laughed Maud.

Again Dr. Hilton looked at her earnestly; he seemed to have a way of talking lightly, and looking earnestly while he did so.

"Do you wonder?" he cried quickly. "I don't; I understand quite well why I have not, and some day I'll tell you."

"Do you? will you?" replied she, surprised. "Very well, I shall certainly remind you, if you don't; you have excited my curiosity now."

"Trust a woman for having her curiosity easily excited by a hint or a straw! However, there really will be something to hear: thereby hangs a tale."

"You will have no difficulty, I should think, in supplying the want in London whenever you choose," continued Maud; "especially if you enumerate all the good things you possess first. I dare say that even among your young lady patients, you might suit yourself, might not you?"

Dr. Hilton laughed and shook his head.

"I hope I may suit myself some day or other," said he. "By-the-bye, Underwood, can you tell me anything of our old friend Fane? Where is he, with that vision of beauty, his wife? Where on earth did the fellow pick up that wonderful creature? and what has he done with her?"

There was a dead silence for a moment, and then it was Maud who replied, quiet and self-possessed:

"He—has gone to Australia," she said in a low voice.

"Gone to Australia!" cried Hilton, startled out of his usual easy *insouciance.* "Gone to Australia! You don't say so! Why, I thought he was one of the London barristers who held his own, and made quite as much of his profession as he cared to do. Does he practise in one of their great cities, or has he turned farmer? And how does that beautiful child like it? Gone to Australia! Fane! Well, really, now, I am very much surprised!"

Maud looked at her brother for help. She was not sure whether she ought to touch on the subject of their friend's domestic troubles. She was astonished to see how white and ghastly Lewes's face was; and then she thought she was mistaken, for as she looked, the colour rushed into and spread over it.

He felt a strong inclination to say out at once, " Fane is dead," and have done with it, and let this lively, chatty Maud bear it all as best she could; but he resisted the inclination, and merely remarked, in as careless a manner as he could, that he believed Mrs. Fane was in Jamaica with her uncle and aunt, Major and Mrs. Cameron.

But then it was Maud's turn to be astonished, and to turn first white and afterwards red, and to exclaim :

" She is in Jamaica ! Why, Lewes, you never told me! How do you know? When did you hear? Is not she at Clapham ?"

The Vicar felt worried and hunted; but tried to behave as he should have done if he had not that day heard of his friend's death.

" I went to Clapham while you were asleep this afternoon. I wanted something to do, and I did that. And there I learned that Freda had gone out to Jamaica."

" Dear me, how very strange !"

" I don't see why it was strange, Maud. She went to Clapham more to wait to hear from her uncle than for any other reason; and her plans would naturally depend on what she heard."

" But now it's my turn, please," cried Dr. Hilton ; "and perhaps you will kindly take compassion on my ignorance, and inform me. Is it a common arrangement for the husband to be so entirely left out of the wife's plans ? Is it usual for the husband to be in Australia and the very young and uncommonly beautiful wife to be first at Clapham and then at Jamaica ? How do you account for *that*, good people ?"

Again Maud looked helplessly at her brother ; and at last he spoke.

" There were some misunderstandings," said

he; " and a temporary separation might be the best plan. The Camerons are sensible people, and their young niece might be happiest with them for a time."

Mr. Underwood really was not aware that he was going to say that about the Camerons till the words were out of his mouth. The fact is, he knew nothing whatever of them; but the words seemed somehow to know that they were the best that could be said under the circumstances, and so they came out of his mouth as if of themselves—a process Freda had partially described in one of her conversations with him, and in which it really does seem as if there is some reality. Of course, it would be very unfair if words had the power of doing this, unless there was something in the lips through which they came which gave that power to them; and yet I do not know what habit lay about the Vicar's lips, from which these words derived it, for he was as simple-minded and straightforward a man as ever stepped. Perhaps it was the concealment that he had practised towards his sister for so long a time with regard to his feelings for Freda, and which must

in the course of daily intercourse have en-
tailed many slight subterfuges upon him.
And yet was he to blame for that? Are we
bound to tell those we live with everything
about ourselves? If we are, are there many
of us who do so?

Dr. Hilton gave a low subdued whistle
when he heard this explanation.

"Phew!" he said softly; "is that how the
matter lies? Verily, these beautiful visions,
these phantoms of delight, are not the best
sort of women, or, at least, don't make the
best wives; but if you *have* such a creature
for your wife, it seems a queer sort of thing
for you to go to Australia, and to send her to
Jamaica." Here he gave another gentle but
slightly prolonged whistle, and added, "However, Fane always had a temper of his own;
that must be confessed, any way."

Maud coloured, hesitated, and glanced at
her brother.

"I don't think Mr. Fane appeared to be
in fault," she said, when she found that
Lewes continued silent.

He, for his part, longed to call out to them
to be quiet—for mercy's sake to hold their

tongues; for Lionel Fane was far beyond all comment of theirs—removed from this earthly sphere of attack and defence—asleep in his Australian grave! But he could not do so; he feared the shock to his sister, and especially at such a moment as this, when she appeared unusually gay and bright. He was not sure whether he could say anything if it was not the whole truth; but after a little reflection he contrived to say:

"There is no good in talking about it. Perhaps the marriage was a mistake. Perhaps there was not much cause for blame to either side. A thorough incompatibility of temper, and neither understanding the other. But it is all over now. God help her!"

Dr. Hilton looked a little surprised at the conclusion of his sentence; and Maud, surprised also, could not refrain from adding, in a low voice:

"And him!"

At which Hilton laughed, and exclaimed:

"Very true, indeed, Miss Underwood. And him! I am glad you have some compassion on us poor men in unhappy marriages, though I am not at all sure that we deserve it; for how a sensible man ever comes to make a mistake and marry the wrong person, is a thing I never yet could understand."

"I dare say you can't," replied the Vicar; and by his manner he evidently considered he had said a sharp thing.

"And I should have thought Fane the last man to do it," persisted Dr. Hilton. "Now, I appeal to Miss Underwood: would you have thought Fane a man to be easily caught? Don't you think he could hold his own against a woman's charms as well, or better, than most of us?"

Maud blushed and hesitated, but she was spared the difficulty of answering an embarrassing question by her brother.

"There is no talk of being caught here," he said, with a calmness that belied his feelings and surprised himself. "Mrs. Fane was a mere child, and she was incapable of trying to catch any one. There was nothing of the kind. He fell in love, poor fellow! Her friends told her to marry him, and she did so, understanding nothing about it. That is the whole history."

"Very likely, when they have tried living apart awhile, they will find it all right when they come together again; though certainly there was no occasion for them to be off to Australia and Jamaica to bring *that* about," said Dr. Hilton cheerfully.

Mr. Underwood shaded his eyes with his hand, and answered not.

"Where and when did you come across them?" asked Maud.

"I caught a glimpse of them on their route from Scotland to Southampton, when they had been married only a week or two. We met at a railway station, and were an hour in each other's company, waiting for a train; at least, he and I were. We smoked our cigars on the platform. I was introduced to her, and had a little chat; that was all. But she was a girl who, once seen, could not be forgotten. Don't you think so, Underwood?"

Underwood stared at him, as if surprised by the question, and then replied, "Yes."

Shortly afterwards Dr. Hilton rose to take his leave. He had come to the hotel to visit a patient there, when he saw and recognised Maud coming out of her sitting-room, and he said he would look in on them again in the morning, as the invalid was ill enough to require daily attendance. Lewes asked him to breakfast, and he accepted the invitation with alacrity.

When he was gone, it seemed to the Vicar, much to his surprise, that Maud was thinking more of him, than of either Lionel or Freda. She began immediately to praise him.

"What a very agreeable man he has grown!" she cried.

"Yes—hasn't he?" replied the Vicar.

"Such easy, pleasant manners, and so much dry humour about him. And he was such a quiet, silent lad in the old days, I never should have expected it. Would you, Lewes?"

"Yes, of course, I suppose so," was the not very relevant answer.

"Why, Lewes, I don't believe you are listening to a word I say."

Lewes started, shook himself, and tried to smile.

"Yes, my dear Maud, I really am; but the fact is, I have got an abominable headache."

Then Maud pitied him and petted him, gave him eau de cologne, begged his pardon for worrying him, and advised him to eat some dinner and go to bed.

"It is the voyage, of course," she said; "and then running off to Clapham in the sunshine, instead of resting. You think you can do anything, Lewes, and that nothing will tire you or make you ill; but indeed it is foolish, and I am always afraid that, some day or other, you will knock yourself up. Do go to bed now, and sleep it off."

"Yes," said the Vicar, with a wan smile; "I believe I had better go to bed."

Sleep it off. That is very pleasant and very good advice; but, unluckily, pleasant and good advice cannot always be followed. If Maud had seen her brother pacing his room in deep distress of mind, even till the small hours in the morning, mourning for his friend, and dismayed as to how and when he should break the sad news of his friend's death to his sister, she would have felt how much easier it was to say " Sleep it off," than to do it.

But Maud knew nothing of all this, and imagined her brother sleeping soundly, while she herself sought repose, with feelings that were unusually bright and cheerful. She had enjoyed her meeting with an old friend, and had thought the time spent in his society had been very agreeably spent ; and she had particularly enjoyed—though that she was not herself conscious of—the something in his manner that seemed to show that his recollection of her was keen. She not only felt that the past evening was pleasant, but she had breakfast-time next morning to look forward to ; and beyond that, perhaps—who knows ?—the renewal of the old intimacy, stretching out into new days.

Maud was still enough of an invalid to often indulge in the habit—condemned by some, approved by others—of breakfasting in bed. Not seldom she found that she was far more capable of useful and healthful exertion during the remainder of the day if she rested for its first hour, and ate her breakfast before she attempted to begin it. Old-fashioned people consider this as a crime, and I myself knew a lady who restricted the breakfast of any one who partook of it in bed, to tea and toast, laying down the principle, that if they were able to eat anything else, they must be able to get up to eat it. Probably she was much fitter to go without substantial food, sitting stoutly at the head of her own break-fast-table after the performance of an elaborate toilette, than the weaker person upstairs, who required nourishment before she could even get up and dress.

Maud Underwood always breakfasted in bed when she liked—which she very often did—and it might naturally be supposed that the day after a journey and a voyage, she would be particularly unfit to rise without food. But such was not the case ; and half-past nine o'clock found her sitting behind the hissing urn, in a pretty muslin dress, with her hair very nicely plaited, and a bright look in her face, awaiting the appearance of her brother and his guest.

The latter came first, and the mutual greetings were very cordial. Dr. Hilton sat beside her, and asked her about her home, its neighbourhood, its occupations and amusements ; so that it was the most natural thing possible for Maud, when praising the Vicarage garden and the surrounding country, to say what pleasure it would give them if he would look in on them some day. The alacrity with which he caught at the idea was gratifying, and she felt herself colouring a little with a curious sort of satisfaction, when she found that, from what he said, he was evidently desirous that a time should be fixed when this looking in might take place. She wondered whether Lewes would be surprised. But Lewes was hospitable; and even if he was a little surprised, she was sure he would be pleased also. So when she found that it was being made plain to her that, for some reasons or other, Dr. Hilton would be able to leave his patients the week after next, she begged that he would use the holiday by spending it in North Wales; and he assured her that nothing would give him greater pleasure.

Just as this matter had been amicably settled between them, Lewes entered the room; but the moment Maud beheld his face, the whole current of her ideas changed.

"Oh, Lewes!" she cried; "how ill you look! You are as white as a sheet. What *is* the matter?"

"It is nothing," he replied, "only I did not *sleep off my headache.*"

"You look as if you hadn't slept all night," said the Doctor with a professional air.

"No, I didn't sleep. I had a headache; that's all. Come, Maud, give me a cup of strong tea, and don't mind my looks; even I may have a headache sometimes."

"Yes, really, that's all," said Dr. Hilton reassuringly to Maud, who appeared anxious and unhappy. "Our friend here is as sound as a bell. Any office would insure his life, only from seeing him. I wish you seemed as healthy as he does."

"I have not been strong for years," she replied, "and I have suffered from rheumatic fevers, which I fancy always leave their traces behind."

He looked scrutinisingly at her, and said:

"If you were my patient, I think I could get rid of them, though."

" Very well, let me become your patient then," she said, smiling. " Take me in hand when you come to Wales." She glanced at her brother. " I am happy to tell you, Lewes, that Dr. Hilton is going to pay us a visit at the Vicarage, in about ten days."

" I am delighted to hear it," replied the Vicar, but without much glow or enthusiasm.

" I shall like to see you in harness, and to hear you preach, old fellow. You were not a parson, and I was not a doctor, when we last parted. I will prescribe for Miss Under-wood's body, and you shall look after my soul."

" Oh, I hope," cried Maud, " that you are not—that you have not—they say that medical men—but I beg your pardon——" She stopped, alarmed at her own temerity, this gentle, good woman.

" I understand," he said gravely and kindly, but still with the little humorous twinkle in his eyes which seldom left them. " No ; not at all. Don't be afraid, and I am very much obliged to you. But I hope I have gone deeply enough into the mysteries of my pro-fession to acknowledge them as mysteries which make those of faith doubly credible. Besides which, I have the advantage of attending church at the Temple, and 'sitting under' that best of good men, Dr. Vaughan, whose sermons have done much for other Londoners, besides lawyers."

"Thank you," was all Maud replied, with a gentle bright look.

He regarded her very kindly indeed.

"There are very useful books, too, published nowadays," said he, "which *face* difficulties, and help one wonderfully to see light. Have you," turning to the Vicar, "met with Mr. Page Robert's books? His 'Reasonable Service' was of the greatest use to *me*."

"I know that, and one other," replied Lewes, "and I heartily wish he had published two dozen volumes instead of two. I think they are quite admirable. I wish I knew the man."

Conversation proceeded very pleasantly, at least between Maud and Dr. Hilton, who occupied her attention so entirely that she scarcely noticed her brother's silence and abstracted manner. The Underwoods were to leave by a mid-day train, so, when breakfast was finished, Maud was obliged to say 'good-bye' to her new-old friend, in order that she might finish her packing and be ready. Dr. Hilton's adieu was really affectionate, and she responded to it with great cordiality.

When he would have shaken hands with Lewes, he looked hard at him and said :

" You are *not* ill, are you ?"

" No," replied the Vicar, " I am *not* ill, but I have something to tell you. I'll walk a bit with you on your way home."

The two men went out of the hotel in silence, and in silence walked down Jermyn Street. They had nearly reached the end of it, and still the Vicar did not speak.

Dr. Hilton was a patient man, but, even for a patient man, the position was unpleasant. " I will give him till I have taken a dozen steps more," thought he to himself, " and then if he doesn't speak, I will." He took his twelve steps, counting them honestly, and, with the thirteenth, he spoke.

" Well, what is it ?" he asked cheerily.

Lewes Underwood stopped, faced him, and instantly answered him :

" I heard last night that Fane is dead."

" Fane dead !" cried Dr. Hilton.

" He was thrown from his horse and killed, somewhere or other in Australia, and it was in consequence of his death that his widow went to Jamaica."

" Then they were not separated at all ?"

" Oh yes, they were. He had left her in England."

" Poor fellow ! What a shocking thing ! I am very sorry for him ; and to think of that beautiful girl being a widow ! and she didn't care for him. Well, I dare say she won't wear her weeds long. Poor Fane ! Poor fellow !"

" My sister is in very delicate health ; any sort of shock or grief has been proved to be very bad for her. I really don't know how to tell her, or what to do about it. Here she is, just come home better, after having been kept so long abroad merely for her health."

Dr. Hilton glanced sideways at him, out of the corners of his eyes.

" She would feel it so much ?" he asked quietly.

" Yes, of course she would ; such a very old friend."

" I remember, long ago," said Dr. Hilton slowly, " that I used to fancy—nay, that I entirely believed—there was an attachment between them."

" Yes—no—nothing of the sort, but a warm friendship, a sufficiently warm friendship to make me very sorry indeed to have to tell her this—in her state of health, you know. Of course I only mean in her state of health."

" I see," said the Doctor, looking at him steadily for a minute, and then walked on for another minute with eyes fixed on the ground. After that he spoke : " If you go home at once, will you come across anybody who will talk about it ? Will she be in the way of hearing it referred to ?"

" Oh no ; nobody will care anything about it, except, indeed, one farmer's wife who knew Freda. *He* is quite unknown in our neighbourhood, poor fellow."

" That farmer's wife could be given a hint, I suppose, to hold her tongue ?"

" Certainly. But still, you know, it would not be possible to keep it always from her."

" No, not always ; but just at first. Let

her settle herself and get over the return home—wait a week or two—that's my advice."

"Well, I dare say it is not bad advice," said the Vicar thoughtfully. "Very likely I may follow it."

"Do," replied the Doctor. "If I were you," he added carelessly, "I wouldn't tell her before—let's say before I run down. My visit will give a change to her thoughts, bring a lot of new ideas into the North Wales life; and after that" (here he again regarded his companion with sidelong glances, out of the corners of his eyes), "after that, may be a good time for letting her hear all about it."

Lewes Underwood was very glad to be advised not to inflict this pain on his sister at present, and very glad to be spared himself, for the present, the pain of having to do so. He felt it was a comfortable thing to talk his difficulties and troubles over with a friend, which for years past he had never had any opportunity of doing, having always to consult with and decide for himself. He began to be glad that they had so unexpectedly met Dr. Hilton, and that he was intending to pay them a visit, in the prospect of which, till that moment, he had taken little pleasure. It seemed to him, though there was nothing striking or brilliant, there was something reliable and comfortable in this man; and the interest he took in their concerns, and the lively manner in which he remembered the old days, was gratifying and pleasant. He looked at his fair, pale, sensible face with satisfaction, and when they shook hands with each other a few minutes later, the pressure Lewes gave was as warm as that which he received from Arthur, and his injunction to him not to disappoint them by forgetting his engagement was almost eager.

And so they went their different ways, Lewes returning sadly, yet with a relieved mind, to the hotel, and Arthur hastening to the performance of his daily duties, but not hastening to them before a momentary pause, during which he looked up to the summer sky, and uttered very earnestly the words of an ordinary grace after meat:

"Thank God for this and all His other mercies."

CHAPTER VIII.

FREDA AGAIN.

A GOOD many months had elapsed since the Vicar and Dr. Hilton parted in Jermyn Street : months that had brought, as months will do, many chances and changes, not only to the people about whom this story treats, but to all the people in the world, and to none, perhaps, more than to some personages for the present staying in a little English watering-place, which we will designate by the letter S.

The hotel in S. was not a large one, but it was comfortable, bright, and pretty. It had its coffee or *table-d'hôte* room, its ladies' drawing-room, and its suites of private apartments, and moreover it stood in gay gardens, which extended to the edge of the esplanade; the esplanade, of course, lay in front of the sea, and on the other side of it, of course, there were terraces of handsome houses.

A gentleman had arrived at S. by the evening mail, and had proceeded at once, as most gentlemen did, to the hotel. He had a good deal of luggage with him. He was a tall, imposing-looking man, and he engaged a private sitting-room as well as a bedroom : sufficient reasons, though he was not accompanied by a valet or groom, why he should be treated with respect, and command the best that the hotel afforded. He arrived too late for the *table-d'hôte*, and ordered dinner in the public room—a mark, I always think, of refinement in the sojourners in hotels, even though they have engaged drawing-rooms, for it is not pleasant to live in the same apartment in which you eat. After changing his dress he came down to his fried sole and cutlet, and found another gentleman in the coffee-room waiting for his dinner also.

This was a young, well-dressed, good-looking, sprightly man, who, after reconnoitring the traveller, asked him in an almost coaxing way whether he was not of the opinion that solitary dull meals were bad for the digestion, and that if two men *had* to dine in the same apartment they might as well eat at the same table and talk, as at different tables and hold their tongues.

"There is something so low in *only* eating; don't you think so?" concluded the sprightly man.

The traveller, whose appearance was rather reserved than sprightly, and who had an air of almost mournful dignity about him, politely assented, and the two sat down to the same table and partook of their *filet de sole* together.

"S. is a charming little place, and full just this minute of no end of nice people," said the sprightly man in a sprightly manner.

"Ah—indeed," replied the other, and then, as if he felt that to be taciturn and to be rude, might under special circumstances be synonymous terms, he added, "The neighbourhood looks pretty."

"*Beautiful*," cried the sprightly one, after emptying a glass of champagne—"first-rate for picnics. I have just returned from one—

ha, ha, ha ! No affront to the picnic, I am very glad to dine again at eight o'clock. Lobster-salad and raspberry-cream at two does *not* content human nature, as it presents itself in the person of your humble servant."

" Picnics are intolerable—worse even than balls," said the traveller ; " they spoil three things—society, scenery, and dinner."

The sprightly man laughed a great deal at this.

" But, mark you," he said, " though I laugh I don't agree. I think all that depends on circumstances. A picnic *may* be delicious, and the one I have just had the honour of forming a component part of, I assure you, my dear sir, was not to be despised."

" **Far** be it from me to despise it," replied the other, " as long as I am not expected to join it."

" If you are not sociable you should not have come to S., for it is sociability itself."

" I have been ill, and came for my health," replied the traveller shortly.

"Ah, the air is balmy, splendid, pretty well, as the Frenchmen would say ; but society is more necessary to health than air itself ; and

S., with all its brilliant reunions, will be of no use to you, if those reunions are to be avoided. Solitude in a crowd, you know, was long ago pronounced to be the only solitude that was really painful."

" If I don't like S. I needn't stay at S.," was the answer, not delivered in a manner encouraging to further advances.

The sprightly man consoled himself for the dulness of his companion by a second helping from a fricassée of chicken, which spoke volumes in favour of the cuisine at the S. hotel.

The traveller ate sparingly, drank more sparingly still, and did all with the air of a man to whom nothing afforded enjoyment, and who most certainly only ate to live. The two men did not seem to be well suited to be companions, even for half an hour, at an inn repast.

" We have delightful dances too," continued the irrepressible sprightly man—" delightful dances—promenades you know they used to be called in the days when our grandmothers were young—those inexpensive, innocent hops, where nothing is thought of but dancing and flirtation—where girls wear those irresistible demi-toilettes, which play the deuce with us poor mortals far more than full dress, and an ease prevails in everything, which furthers a flirtation better than aught beside. Believe me, sir, those wonderful little conclusions to the turn on the esplanade—dances, which are not balls, and which are unaccompanied by sit-down suppers—are the inventions of youth and joy themselves."

" I *have* been at such," replied the traveller gloomily, " but it seems to me as long ago as if it had been in another era and another world. And girls and dancing, youth and joy—all the things, in fact, that you converse about—appear to me equally far off."

" Why, my dear sir, you can't be older than I am !" cried the sprightly man, amazed and commiserative. " What a pity—what a very great pity !"

" Is it ?" said the traveller, grimly. " I don't know. Truth, I suppose, is better than delusion."

" Well now," cried the sprightly one, laying down his napkin and pushing himself on his chair a step back from the table, " it is a very good thing that I have, on the whole, eaten a very good dinner—for do you know you've taken away my appetite completely, you have indeed."

He laughed as he spoke, and got up, and the other followed his example—at least, he got up; he did not laugh.

He was a very handsome man, but pale, and looked in bad health ; his eyes were a bright brown, by no means as dark as might have been expected from the rest of his colouring, and therefore giving a peculiar expression to his face ; his nose was manly and well-formed, but nothing very unusual or striking ; but his mouth and chin, not in any way hidden by the short moustache and well-trimmed whiskers, were the features most unlike those of his fellow-men, and giving the character that it bore, to his face. The lips were small and clean-cut, the upper short and habitually slightly curled, firm and obstinate in expression, though exceedingly handsome in shape ; and the cleft chin, slightly projecting, increased ten-fold the expression of the mouth, and verily was the chin of a man who having once made up his mind did not know how to change it.

His companion looked at him with more admiration than men commonly bestow on each other, and with even, perhaps, a dash of envy.

" I wonder," he said, " you dislike all those sort of things, for I should say they would like you—rather. Shall we take a stroll and a smoke ?"

They went out on the esplanade ; the summer twilight was still bright, and seemed almost to mock the beautiful moon that hung over the sea. I do believe that some moons are more beautiful than others—this one was calm, brilliant and preternaturally large.

" Are the large Indian moons as serene as of old,
  When as children we gathered the moonbeams for gold ?"

" Well, I have seen moons half over the world, and I don't know that any are better than those at home," said the traveller.

" To tell you the truth, I don't much care about moons myself," replied his companion confidentially. " I never did. I like sunlight, and if I haven't got that, I like firelight and gas. The only good of a moon is to smoke a cigar by, when a smoking-room is too hot, or it's too early in the evening to light it up."

They strolled on, conversing rather idly in this way, and passing between the sea and the terraces of houses. The traveller looked at the sea and the moon, and the sprightly man looked at the houses.

He suddenly paused before one of these.

" There," he said, " in that house lives the leader of fashion and amusement here—the most beautiful woman I ever saw—a young widow, and, by Jove! there she is !"

Even as he spoke the words, two girls had stepped out on the balcony above them, and leaning on the balustrades gazed out on the calm blue waters rippling softly under the light of the moon. One of these young ladies was pale and slight, nice-looking and interest-ing. The traveller's eyes passed carelessly over her form and figure in its flowing blue draperies, and were riveted on the other girl. She was dressed in some airy shining black material, and her arms and neck shone through it with dazzling whiteness ; her form was perfectly graceful, and her face faultlessly beautiful, with all the *beauté de diable* (that of extreme youth), its lilies and roses and its unstained innocent joys, joined to that of the most ideal womanhood.

For one moment the eyes of the traveller rested on this radiant vision, at first with simple inquiry, and afterwards with an expression of recognition which held in it an element of madness. And then he turned round and walked rapidly away. His companion heard him mutter something as he did so, and as he had spoken of bad health and was pale and thin and rather dreamy in his ideas, he made no doubt that he was seized with some sudden illness, and feeling sorry for him, he followed in his wake, willing to assist him if assistance was necessary.

The other walked straight to the hotel, and to the bar, where he addressed the officiating damsel, asking if there was a night train.

" Yes—at nine twenty."

" Very well, get me my bill; I am going by it."

The young lady expressed her regret; she had understood the gentleman had engaged rooms and intended to stay. Shall she order his luggage downstairs ?

"Yes—no—it may remain. I may return —at least—" here he stopped and appeared for an instant to commune with himself in deep, though rapid cogitation.

The young man who had followed him, stood staring behind him. "Dear me," he said, "I thought you were going to stay here for your health."

"And you find I'm not," replied he roughly.

And so saying, he passed rapidly upstairs to his room.

Meantime the two girls stood on the balcony and gazed out into the beautiful night—for the summer night was stealing on apace.

The one in blue said suddenly : "Well, that was the handsomest man I ever saw ; but we frightened him. He looked up at us, and then he gave a great start, almost a jump ; and then he almost ran away, and Mr. Jennings after him."

"Oh, Mr. Jennings — I'm tired of Mr. Jennings, and I hate handsome men !" replied the girl in black.

"Are you tired of this place, Freda ?

There is a sameness about life here that might tire some, I think."

" Oh no ; oh, not one bit. I am never tired of that endless blue sea, stretching always on till it melts into sky, so that there *is* no end to it; who could tire of that ? and then the moonlight on it as if it never could cease either—only it does."

" And the life ? are you not yet tired of picnics, and dances, and esplanades, and admiration ?"

Freda shook her lovely head gently to and fro.

" Not one bit," she cried ; " I don't expect ever to tire of them—never while it is all out of doors.   I hate a house and I hate winter. We'll go somewhere, Corabel, when summer is over, somewhere where houses are not needed and winter can't overtake us."

" Poor Mr. Jennings," laughed Corabel ; " then you are only tired of *him* ?"

" Only tired of him," echoed Freda, and echoed the laugh also.   " I *do* tire of men uncommonly soon ; I wish I didn't. It would be nicer if I didn't, because I have so much to do with men."

"Are you engaged for *all* the dances on Thursday?"

"No, I have taken a new plan; I am free every fourth dance; I make no engagements for every fourth dance, and that gives me a chance of a stranger. I do like a stranger—I am never tired of a stranger—not even if it is a man."

Corabel laughed. "And I never like strangers till they cease to be strangers. Just when you tire of them, I begin to like them."

"Oh, Corabel, I have remembered what I had forgotten!"

"And what is that? why, Freda, you look ready to cry."

"Oh, Corabel, poor Benjamin! I am so sorry—so very sorry. I promised to see him to-day and to take him some flowers—and I didn't! That picnic made me forget, and I would rather have lost twenty picnics than have disappointed poor Benjamin. Let us go now directly — let us get our hats and run."

"But, Freda, it is so late; and it is a good way off, and not a nice street."

"What does that matter? think of the joy

in his face. What do lateness and good
ways and streets signify compared with his
poor white face ?"

" He will be asleep."

" Ah—will he ? I don't think so; he
tosses about and can't sleep till late—so late.
And if he *is*, what a lovely dream he will
think us, appearing suddenly with flowers.
Do as you like, dear, but I am going, and
going instantly too."

" Of course you are, if you choose : you
always do what you choose. Oh yes, I am
coming with you, that is of course also : I
also always do what you choose."

So Freda and Corabel put on their hats
and wrapped mantles round their pretty
shoulders, and set off with light rapid steps
towards a street that, as Corabel said, was
not a nice one, away from the sea at the back
of the town.

The street reached, they stopped at the
door of a poor mean little house where Freda
tapped softly and, without waiting for an
answer, entered. The room inside was sad
and squalid-looking; it contained only two
inmates—a woman sitting knitting by the

light of a single tallow candle which made a dim melancholy illumination, mixing as it did, and at the same time contrasting painfully, with the summer twilight; and lying in a small bed, a child with a white face and preternaturally large and bright, wide-opened eyes. There were the signs of tears on his pale cheeks, but as the door moved and Freda, in her shining airy black dress, a light white shawl wrapped over her shoulders, her exquisite face smiling out from under her tiny black hat and feather, and carrying in her hands a bouquet of splendid sweet-scented hot-house flowers, glided into the room, a radiant vision of beauty, a visitant indeed from a higher and a better sphere, he burst into a sad little fit of shrill laughter, and clapped feebly together his hands with their long skeleton-like fingers, crying out as he did so : "There, mammy, wasn't I right not to go to sleep? the lady's come."

The woman rose astonished from her seat.

"Who'd have thought it?" she said. "Well, well, they do say, that when they're on the edge of another world, they know more about this one than common; but I never believed it afore. You're kindly welcome, my lady; and poor Ben has been looking for you all day, and wouldn't go to sleep now, because he still expected you."

Freda smiled gently on the woman, and went with her light dancing steps at once to the sick boy's side, holding the flowers to his face, burying it in them for a moment, and then placing them in his outstretched eager hands.

"Did you want me, Benny?" she said, stroking his white cheeks with her rosy-tipped taper finger.

"I just did," replied he in voice and manner as if he indeed "just had;" "half an hour ago I *longed* for you, so I thought you must come."

Freda glanced almost triumphantly at Corabel.

"And that was *it*," she cried, "that was what brought me; you longed so, Benny, that I felt it, and *had* to come; that often happens, and I am *so glad* it does. I *am* so glad that people feel and know about each other when they are not together; it's useful, it's nice, and, in some sort of a manner, it's very pleasant to think of."

"I'll tell you what I mean to do," cried Benny with exultation; "it's such a good plan. When I'm in heaven, I mean to long for you just that way, and then you'll have to fetch yourself dead and come up to me. Oh! won't it be pretty to see you fly in !"

And he clapped his poor bony hands again, and again gave his little burst of shrill, mournful-sounding laughter.

Freda looked quite appalled, and actually grew rather pale.

"Oh no, don't; please, *please* don't, Benny, I don't wish it; I don't want to fetch myself dead; I don't want to go to heaven. Promise me you won't, Benny; if you love me, promise it, quick !"

Benjamin seemed greatly disappointed.

"I promise," he said. "I mind you always, and I'll mind you in heaven; but I thought it *was* a good plan."

Freda breathed more freely again.

"There's my dear boy," she said, imprinting a light kiss on his cheek. "Now go to sleep, my pet, and dream nice, pretty dreams about the box of tin soldiers, all painted blue and red, with swords in their hands, I shall bring you the next time I come."

" It's very good of your ladyship, I'm sure," said the woman. " And he takes the tea and the jelly, and he'd be dead now if it wasn't for you."

" No I wouldn't," cried Benny manfully. " It's not she keeps me out of heaven. She's good, and she'd let me go to the good place ; she wouldn't try to keep me in the bad place, where I'm sick. Why don't we all go to heaven together right off ? Why was it naughty of old Joe to hang himself ? And why are we told not to murder ? People *ought* to kill each other, or leastways themselves, and go to the good place straight off."

He had begun to speak with animation, but he seemed getting tired and sleepy, and murmured at the last words almost as if he did not understand their meaning.

Freda looked round her helplessly.

" Oh dear," she cried, " I think he's right. Why isn't he right ? Why don't we ? Why oughtn't we ?"

Then Corabel seemed to think she had been

silent long enough. She stepped to the other
side of the bed, and murmured a few words
like prayer over the sick child, and said softly,
" God sent us here, and we have to stay as
long as He pleases, and in His own time He
takes us to heaven, if we try to be good, and
are patient and not in a hurry."

This Benny seemed to understand, sleepy as
he was, for he smiled at Freda, and whisper-
ing " She's good, she's not in a hurry," he
shut his eyes and went to sleep.

Freda put her finger on her lips and said
" Hush !" nodded her head kindly to the
poor woman, and moved softly on tip-toe out
of the house.

When she was safely outside she breathed
more freely, and helped herself to do so by a
great sigh.

" Oh, I wish he wouldn't," she cried ; " he
frightens me. I shall have to give up seeing
him if he talks that way ; he frightens me
very much. They don't all do it, you know.
Uncle Cameron didn't, not one bit. He went
on just as usual, only getting not so well or
strong ; and he read the newspapers, and never
talked the least wild or said shocking things ;

and he smoked every day, and the very last
evening aunt and I played whist with him
with a dummy, and then he died in his sleep
afterwards. I do think that is much nicer,
don't you, Corabel? Oh!"—with a shiver—
" don't let us talk of such things at all; it's
growing quite dark, and it feels horrid. Let's
run, or walk fast, like running, and get home
as quick as possible, and light up all the gas,
and dance. We can waltz together, you
know, quite well, and I can sing while we
waltz."

And Freda began singing, in a low, sweet
voice :

> " Life is for dancing
>   Lightly and fairily ;
> Seasons advancing
>   Pirouet airily.
> Some dance on roses,
>   Some while leaves fall to rest ;
> Winter's white snow is
>   Fairer than all the rest."

" Hush, Freda! don't sing; people will
wonder at you. We are just close to the
railway station now, and we shall meet
people."

" I don't mind meeting people," said

32—2

Freda composedly, "and I am sure they don't mind meeting me. They never seem to mind it one bit. I think they rather like it."

" Do be quiet, there's a dear," said Corabel.

" You are always for being quiet, and it's unlucky, for it's just the one thing I never can be. I can be anything else almost, but I can't be quiet. I'd really rather not be alive at all, than be alive and quiet. That's a fact, Corabel, and I think you might know it by this time."

" Oh, Freda, do come on; there is that handsome man again who was with Mr. Jennings, and he did look at you so."

" Where was he? Let me see him too."

" He has just turned in at the railway station; you are too late."

" As if I cared. If I did I would follow him immediately. You have fallen in love with that handsome man, but I have not. I hate men, as I told you, and I wonder you don't hate them too. If you like to run in and take another look at him, I'll wait for you here."

And Freda came to a full stop, and stood

motionless in the centre of the footpath. Corabel put her hand through her arm and led her forcibly on.

"Don't be foolish," she said severely. " Come home before you've collected a crowd round you, if you please."

" But I like a crowd, especially when it's collected round *me !*" cried the incorrigible girl, allowing her friend, however, to lead her slow and apparently reluctant steps towards home.

" You like everything that you shouldn't like, and nothing that you should."

" *Vide* handsome men," cried Freda, and burst into a peal of silvery laughter.

CHAPTER IX.

AT A BALL.

IT was not long since Freda and her friend had returned from Jamaica. Delighted at first with all the wonders and novelties of the island, Freda had declared that she would live all her life there, and that a life spent there must be twice as long as anywhere else, because it would be one of perfect happiness. Very soon, however, her uncle, Major Cameron's, failing health turned her thoughts and attentions from outer things, and, slightly neglected by the wife who had lived only for ease and enjoyment, and had been inseparable from him as long as they could share ease and enjoyment together, he found in Freda the most charming of companions and nurses. She was as tender and as helpful as she had been at the Vicarage, and when her uncle died she mourned him sincerely.

After that she did not get on so well with her aunt, who, having been always accustomed to consider her as a child, and to dispose of her just as she liked, did not understand the married Freda, or the manner in which she asserted her separate being. Corabel did not like Mrs. Cameron—a frivolous woman, who might pass muster as a happy wife, but made an intolerable widow.

"It is not pleasant," cried Freda, "and why shouldn't it be pleasant? It *is* so foolish not to be pleasant. Let us sail away somewhere, Corabel, and be as happy as the day's long. Shall we sail away to another island, some bright little isle of our own, in a blue summer ocean, far off and alone? Oh, shall we, Corabel?"

"Yes, yes!" answered Corabel, with unusual eagerness, "and let that island be— England!"

But Freda turned up her pretty nose at

that, as if no sensible person *could* think of sailing away to England.

"England!" she cried, "but that would be such a very slow thing to do, quite commonplace. We'd much better go somewhere far off."

"Alas! England is far off, I think," replied Corabel.

"Some place *more* unusual than Jamaica, not less," said Freda dogmatically. "I don't wish to see England again for ever so long. I'd like to sail round the world first. At any rate, I'll go a good bit farther. Aunt Fanny means to settle in Jamaica, I think, so I won't. We shall be good friends enough, I dare say, in different islands, but we don't do very well in the same one; so let's get out a map of the world, Corabel, and choose an island; any one will do as long as it isn't near Australia."

Freda's plans, however, of choosing an island came to nothing. The climate of Jamaica did not agree with her; she got fever, and though it appeared to be trifling, it weakened her, and then came a relapse, and then another relapse on that, till she was at last confined to her bed, and did not leave it for some weeks. She was never seriously ill, and never lost her spirits, but the doctor who attended her said it was imperatively necessary that she should return to England as soon as she was strong enough to travel. If she remained in Jamaica she would have fever after fever, and if she lived at all, would be an invalid for life ; and England was by far the best climate for her to recover her strength in, even if it had not been her native air. Freda pouted at this, and was inclined to rebel.

" I don't believe it is my native air," she said ; " and if it is, it was only by accident. My father and mother moved about everywhere. I believe I was born at St. Petersburg, or if I wasn't I might just as well have been."

" No you were not," replied Mrs. Cameron. " You were born at Dover."

" Then that makes the sea my native air, and the sea's everywhere, so I may just go where I like."

However, doctors are despotic, and this doctor had his own way, even though it was

Freda who was his patient. Mrs. Cameron was not at all sorry to say good-bye to Mrs. Fane, whom she did not find as manageable as Miss Freda had been, and as soon as the girl was convalescent, she and Corabel returned to England.

When they arrived there, with the world all before them where to choose from, they found it extremely difficult to make a choice. At last Freda seized on a " Bradshaw," and declared that they would go to the first place she opened upon, and read off the page at once.

" Honest as the day, you know, Corabel. Whatever catches my eye the very *first instant*, I shall sing out loud, and there we'll go."

" But it *is* so foolish," remonstrated Corabel, " when it may be some horrid place."

" Then we needn't stay there, you silly ; we *must* go there, but we needn't stay a minute."

" Oh, Freda, how foolish ! Why *should* we go ?"

" Because we *must*, Corabel ; and so it's best to be resigned and cheerful. Let us do it between us ; if *you*'ll be resigned, *I*'ll be cheerful."

" It requires a good deal of resignation to live with you, Freda."

" That's because you haven't got a well-disciplined mind, my dear. I'm trying to train you as well as I can, and by the time you are forty-two I think you'll have learned to submit without a groan to the inevitable."

" Meaning you," cried Corabel. " I'm sure you are inevitable."

" Where's ' Bradshaw ?' Oh, here we are ; very well—one, two, three, and——" Here she opened the paper volume and excitedly uttered the name of S——.

" Very well ; S—— it is, and S—— it must be," she remarked coolly. " Now, then, Corabel, if anything ever was exciting, this is ; to find out what and where S—— is. I hope it's a real place, and not a trick of 'Bradshaw's.' If I had to make a railway guide, what tricks I *would* play ; but 'Bradshaw' is rather matter-of-fact generally."

The two girls were quite astonished when they discovered that S—— was a prettily situated watering-place, famed for its salubrity, that anybody might like to visit, and just now at the height of its season.

" It is more luck than you deserve," said Corabel.

" Yes, I've heard you say that before ; and it is not only impossible, personally speaking, but it always sounds to me profane."

" Profane !"

" Yes, I'm rather particular, I know, and you're careless.   I don't think you mean any wrong, but you're careless, and I am sorry for it.   It's a sort of flying in the face of Providence, as if anybody could have more luck than they deserve.   I know you are not very lucky, Corabel, but you should always comfort yourself with the idea that that is because you don't deserve to be lucky, and that if you did you would."

And so the two friends went to S——.

Cora Bell or Corabel, as she was now invariably called, like everybody else who came near Freda, loved her dearly, and did, in the main, whatever Freda pleased; but she sometimes found fault with her, often gave her advice, and, it cannot be doubted, exerted, though perhaps unknown to either of them, a beneficial influence over her extraordinary young friend.   The two girls read, played, sang, drew, laughed and talked together, and led a happy, pleasant life. But it would be too much to say that either was altogether in the confidence of the other. Freda knew very little of Corabel's affairs or existence before she had met her at Clapham. She knew that she was an orphan, and that her income was very small, so that she had in some manner to eke it out by her own exertions. Freda gave her nothing in money, and in every way treated her as an equal; paid all her expenses, and lavished presents upon her, so that by these means Corabel was able to dress herself and pay for her own washing. Freda behaved to her very affectionately, and talked to her on all subjects save one. The episode of her marriage she never by any chance alluded to; the name of her husband never passed her lips. It almost might seem as if Freda had forgotten that she had ever been married. She was called Mrs. Fane, and she still wore black, only one year having elapsed since that unfortunate husband's death; but the black was now everything that was pretty, fashionable, and becoming, and nothing could be more becoming to Freda than her velvet, silk, or gauzy robes of that sombre hue, which set off the splendour of her complexion to the very greatest advantage.

Freda had got into no scrapes and no difficulties. Everybody liked her when they looked at her, and loved her when they knew her. And liking and love are great helps in keeping people out of scrapes and difficulties. Many blamed her, and some even condemned her, but they liked or loved her notwithstanding. Her method of choosing a place to " go to " was certainly not a usual one, and a large majority of readers will consider that an existence governed by such principles, or want of principles, must be fraught with dangers; but perhaps methodical principles are *not* as necessary in the minor details of life as a large majority consider them; in some cases even, perhaps life would be more agreeable, and not more dangerous, without them than with them. At all events Freda had hitherto, since her widowhood, done remarkably well; and this visit to S——, so recklessly arranged, had turned out a grand success.

I am not altogether advocating her mode

of choosing a residence, but it may not have been a worse one than the reasons that rule methodical existences, and which, I think, seem often framed on purpose to sacrifice all the joyousness of life to the most petty and unimportant, the most trumpery and puerile details. In some houses everything has to give way to the dinner hour; and it is thought wise and rational that everything *should* give way to the dinner hour, which is the most immovable of feasts. Is it necessary to make any comment on such houses as these? And yet they would, in ordinary minds, be held above —as undoubtedly they hold themselves above —those houses where the hour of dining is elastic, and yields to everything else, though as good a dinner is provided at the conveniently irregular hour as in those houses where it is inconveniently regular.

To return from this digression to the actual life of my very irregular heroine. When the Thursday night came—Thursdays were real balls, at least every alternate entertainment deserved that name rather than that of the informal meetings that Mr. Jennings so

greatly delighted in—when the Thursday
night came, Freda was in that little flutter
which is natural to the girl-heart at the
prospect of a ball.

"It is very odd to me, Corabel," she said,
when they went upstairs to dress—to dress!
what a pleasant sound that is to some pretty
little rosy, shell-like ears, what an utterly
tiresome one to ears that are older and
sadder!—"that you never seem to mind."

"To mind?—what, Freda?" answered the
other, slightly startled by the vagueness of
the charge.

"Why, balls and things; you are quite
quiet and calm always. You don't care about
dressing or dancing, or anything; you just
do it—and you do it just as composedly as at
Clapham you performed your duties, and not
with one atom more go!"

"Do I?" replied Corabel, smiling; but
perhaps her smile was a trifle sad. "Indeed
I am not ungrateful, my dear; my path has
fallen on pleasant places—my life is very,
very different from what it was at Clapham,
and I recognise it as such, and am thankful
and glad."

The last word was spoken after a moment's pause, and as if a moment's self-consultation as to whether it could be truly uttered, and then it was spoken firmly, and with a ring in the voice.

" Are you *glad*, Corabel ?" answered Freda wistfully. " *I* am so glad at and of everything ; but you never seem *girl*-glad. Are you girl-glad, Corabel ? Ah !" she cried, suddenly facing her friend, and wringing her hands with a gesture half defiant, half despairing, " does it not seem as if I was the girl and you the *widow ?*"

It was the first time since the day or two that immediately followed the death of her husband, that Freda had ever referred to that event, even so much as she had done now, or spoken of herself as a widow.

Corabel, startled and touched, threw her arms round her, and kissed her tenderly ; and, though her words applied to her own sorrows —from which, or their like, she exempted Freda—her thoughts were full of Freda alone.

" There are heart-widows, my dear one," she said gently. " Thank God, you are not one."

Freda looked at her earnestly, and the clock struck nine.

"We must dress, or we shall be late," cried Corabel; and she went quickly into her room, and shut the door, as if anxious to stop the conversation.

Freda's dress that evening was lovely and becoming; waves of black tulle, scattered with glittering dewdrops, floated about her; silver leaves rested on her bosom, looped up her draperies, and crowned her splendid hair. Her beauty shone out glorious from among them—a beauty to startle, to delight, to subdue.

As the two girls entered the ball-room, which they did at a fashionably late hour, when the most part of Freda's subjects were assembled, a suppressed murmur greeted their appearance—a sound to which they had become accustomed. A dozen men advanced to meet them, and the waltz that was being rather languidly danced came to a close, perhaps sooner than it would otherwise have done. Freda moved forward with bright eager grace, when she felt a slight deterring force acting on her person, and was aware

that a foot must be resting on her train. It
caused her steps to pause suddenly, and she
turned hastily round. The delinquent was a
tall, distinguished-looking man, with a great
quantity of light curling hair, a magnificent
fair beard, tinged with red, that almost concealed his face, and a pair of brilliant, dark
eyes, which as she turned fixed themselves
upon Freda.

" I beg your pardon," he said, and he spoke
with a slightly foreign accent. He withdrew
his foot, and he said nothing more.

Freda gazed at him so earnestly, that he
raised his eyes again and looked at her, then
she dropped hers and blushed. She bent her
head with the easy grace that pervaded
always every movement of Freda's, and,
moving on, was the next moment whirling
round the room in the waltz.

When the dance was over she eagerly
sought Corabel.

" See !" she cried, showing her card, " do
you see my fourth dance ? Wasn't it lucky ?
All my fourth dances I shall keep for *him*.
Only look, I have put a big ✠ to them to
mark it ! I wonder why I put a cross, Cora-

bel?" she added thoughtfully, and as if not quite pleased.

"With him? with whom?" was the rational if not quite sympathetic answer.

"Why, the stranger to be sure—the man who trod on my train. Is it possible you did not look at him—did not notice him? Ah, well! but you know *I* love strangers."

"He has asked you then? He has been introduced?"

"Oh no; but of course he will," replied Freda simply.

Corabel laughed.

"Suppose he didn't!" said she, a little spitefully.

"Oh, but they all do, and why shouldn't *he*? I looked at him, and I think I smiled. I must have smiled, I think; I felt so smiling. He is sure to come."

"I did give him a glance," said Corabel, "when I saw he was treading on your dress. He is a very distinguished, unusual-sort-of-looking man."

"I think I have dreamt of him," replied Freda very thoughtfully; then raising her eyes with a half-scared look, "Oh, I wonder

what I mean! It is only because I love
strangers. You know I love strangers, Corabel."

"Yes, Freda," said Corabel calmly; "I
know you do."

Then Freda had to dance again, and a bevy
of partners surrounded her, imploring for
every dance for which she had not a name
marked on her card. When asked for the
fourth, as she was by several, she always
said she was engaged for it; and she said it
in good faith, for it never for an instant
occurred to her as possible that the tall distinguished-looking man, to whom she had
given a look, and even as she believed a
smile, would not ask to be introduced to her.
But wonders never *do* cease, and Freda's
nineteen summers could not save her from
new experiences. The handsome stranger
took no notice of her, did not come near her,
and never requested or obtained an introduction at all.

Freda was greatly astonished. Then she
grew angry, and after that she felt unaccount-
ably depressed. When the fourth dance
began, she was actually sitting out partner-

less, and it seemed to her as if the world was coming to an end. What could it mean? How could it have happened? And the stranger was actually standing opposite to her, and saw that she sat there and was not dancing, and still he did not approach her. What could it mean? Who could he be? What was he made of? Freda had never felt so interested in anybody in her whole life before, or thought about any man—not even a stranger—for so many consecutive minutes.

However, this state of affairs could not last. There were plenty of men who were not dancing, and they, with Mr. Jennings at the head of them, came eagerly towards her.

"Why, you said you were engaged for this dance!" cried two or three voices.

"You refused *me!*" said Mr. Jennings reproachfully.

"Why do you tell me so?" replied Freda calmly. "It is not so many minutes ago. Do you think I have lost my memory that I should forget it?"

"I think you are very cruel—that is all I think. Why do you treat me so unkindly? Will not you dance with me?"

Freda reflected.

" Who is that tall man with the big beard standing just opposite to us ?" she asked abruptly.

No one knew ; they all asked each other, but no one knew.

" He came to the hotel this morning—that is all I know about him," said Mr. Jennings ; " and he appears acquainted with nobody. Probably he expects friends who have not yet come ; he will join their party, and then we shall find out all about him."

" Find out all about him !" cried she disdainfully. " How low ! Who wants to *find out ?* Finding out is horribly mean."

" Oh, of course, I didn't intend *that*, Mrs. Fane. But will not you dance with me ? will you really not dance with me ? Only listen to the music ! Did you ever hear anything so exhilarating ! Surely you can't sit still !"

" Yes, I will dance with you," replied Freda, and she stood up to do so ; but it seemed to herself that she had spoken the words quite sadly.

She took two turns, and then paused in

the waltz, where she was obliged to stand close to the stranger.

"I am tired to-night," she said to Mr. Jennings; "get me a glass of iced water, will you? I will wait here till it comes."

Her partner flew to obey her, and Freda stood by the stranger's side, but he took no notice of her, and did not even seem conscious of her presence. He was watching the dancers, and Freda watched him stealthily, and felt inexpressibly piqued.

"It does not even know I am alive," she said to herself; "it can't be a real man—it is a figure dressed up!"

Mr. Jennings returned with the iced water, and Freda felt the greatest inclination to fillip a drop or two of it airily into the stranger's face.

"If I were only a child," she sighed to herself, "I might do that or anything else— children may do anything, and *nobody* minds! Ah! the pity of it is that we are not all of us children. Growing up is a mistake."

"I think I shall go home," she said suddenly to Mr. Jennings.

"Go home!" cried he, as shocked and

astonished as if home was the last place any one would ever go to; "why on earth should you do *that*? Are you ill?"

"I never was better in my life; but it *is* so stupid! Don't you think it's horribly stupid?"

"No, I don't. I never enjoyed myself more, and you only say so to chaff me. Of course it is not stupid when I am dancing with you."

"Oh, fiddle-de-dee!" said Freda; "don't begin complimenting—it's wretched stuff, and I'm so tired of it!—so tired!" she repeated pitifully. "I wish I was out of doors in a wood—deep down in a wood, with only birds and flowers. I was once; I was lost there. Oh, why did I ever come away? Why did anybody find me?"

"And who did find· you?" inquired Mr. Jennings, much interested; "who was that benefactor to mankind in general?"

"Somebody you wouldn't care about," cried she, quite in earnest; "the best man I ever knew anywhere in the whole course of my life—a clergyman. I wish he was here now. I do wish he was here now. Why shouldn't he be ?   I declare I'll write to him the first thing to-morrow, and invite him—and Maud too."

" Oh, there is a Maud, too, is there ?" replied he, considerably relieved.   " His wife, of course."

" No, you wise guesser ; not his wife, of course.   He isn't married at all—not the least bit.   Maud is his sister—his sweet, pale sister.   Maud is very nice, but he is nicer."

" It's very unkind of you to sing his praises to me, Mrs. Fane ; you do it on purpose.   But I'm glad he is only a clergyman ; I am indeed !"

" Only a clergyman !" cried Freda, with flashing eyes ; " and what can there be better or higher than a clergyman, if he is a real one and not a make-believe ? Most clergymen are make-believes, but this man is real—he is an out-and-outer !"

" He was a very lucky fellow to find you in the wood, Mrs. Fane.   May one ask what he did with you ?"

" He took me home to his sister, and I pretended to be a servant, and nursed her.

It was sweet—it was heavenly ! Why are
things ever over ? Why do we go on and
on, while they don't, till it seems as if they
could not have been, or as if we must be
somebody else ? Oh, I hope I am not going
to get tired of my life !" she added all of a
sudden in a panic.

Freda was not talking for effect, nor for
the stranger to hear, for she had forgotten all
about him. She was not thinking of Mr.
Jennings either; but was in reality commun-
ing with herself, though she appeared to be
talking to him. Some touch, she knew not
what, or how, had been given to her thoughts,
and sent them back into the past with a wistful longing for days that could never be recalled. What days can be recalled ? None ;
only their ghosts may come back to you, and
what is more dreary than the ghost of a dead
day ? Alas ! is there any one who would
voluntarily raise that saddest of all ghosts—
the ghost of a day that is done ?

Then Mr. Jennings entreated her to " give
him another turn."

" It is hardly fair ; you know it isn't. This
is my waltz, and the next you'll fly away with

somebody else. You might give me just another turn."

"Is dancing everything?" cried she, with flashing eyes; "were we born only to dance? Wasn't I telling you *thoughts?* Are they nothing? Oh yes! very well, to be sure. I forgot you were only Mr. Jennings—I did indeed."

And then she smiled a little—not at all offensively, and held out both her hands to him, saying sweetly:

"Of course you can't help it. Let us dance, by all means."

And so they began to dance again; Mr. Jennings not quite certain whether he was pleased or not.

When they waltzed off from his neighbourhood, the stranger, who had heard every word that passed between them, broke out into a short laugh. It was quite involuntary, and he checked it as soon as he knew what he was doing.

Freda had looked over her shoulder at him as she went away, with Mr. Jennings' arm round her. He was not conscious of the look, and their eyes did not meet. Still she

saw that he laughed, and a bright colour stole
into her cheeks. Was he laughing at her, or
with her ? Many sensitive hearts have asked
this question before, with a tremulous earnestness that seems, to those whom a laugh does
not happen to touch, quite out of proportion
to the occasion. But to Freda the experience
was an unusual one. She laughed at people
as much as ever she liked, but it never occurred to her that they could laugh at her in
return ; and few were more indifferent to, or
even unconscious of, the opinions of their
fellow-creatures than Freda. She had a
general idea, born of the universal admiration she received, that everybody liked her ;
but beyond that she inquired or thought
nothing, being far more occupied with what
she thought of people than with what they
thought of her. Here, however, was a man
whose appearance, or something about him,
she did like—who had in fact made, at first
sight, an impression upon her she was little
accustomed to, and which was as pleasant to
her as it was new, for excitements are pleasant to the young and careless ; and now,
wonderful to relate, this man did *not* like her,

did not seem to care a straw about her, or to be aware even of her existence. What could she do? What could anybody do in such a wonderful, unparalleled state of affairs as this?

What she did do was to waltz with Mr. Jennings; but while she waltzed she thought only of the stranger, and while she thought of him, she cast hasty little glances over her shoulder at him. Was it possible that he would stay in S——, join in the society, go to the dances, yet never be introduced to her, so that they should continue " strangers yet " through it all?

After a while, Freda lost sight of this provokingly interesting man, and supposed he had left the ball-room.

" Well, he can't have enjoyed himself, at any rate," she said with satisfaction, " or he never would have gone home so early."

And so she danced with all those who were dying to dance with her, and forgot the one who did not think about her, who had not cared to be introduced, and had left the room where SHE was, an hour after entering it.

All of a sudden, while pausing herself to

take breath, towards the end of the evening, she saw him again, and he was waltzing.

She was astonished to find that her heart was beating a little faster than usual. Although taking a moment's breathing space, she had no idea she had been dancing enough for *that.*

She saw him distinctly, but at first she could not distinguish who his partner was. She looked again and again, but could only see white draperies floating about him as he glided round and round. Then came a turn, when she saw the lady his arm supported quite clearly.

Would wonders never cease? It was Corabel!

Corabel, who danced little, and never with strangers. She danced little, because she did not care for dancing. Every one who knew her asked Corabel, and, in a mild way, liked her society; but few, almost none, begged for an introduction to her. There was nothing striking about her. How was it possible that this had come about?

Freda was unaffectedly astonished. To the best of her belief, the stranger had not danced before that night; he most certainly had not wished to be introduced to *her*, though she had given him every opportunity; and now there he was, waltzing with Corabel.

At first the sensation Freda experienced when she saw this, was a strange, new, and painful one. Yes, in its very strangeness and newness, it was actually painful; though why it should be painful, she had not the least idea. But afterwards, when she reflected a little, she was glad. This was something to interest and excite. She should hear all about him—who he was, what manner of man he was, what he talked of, and also how the introduction had come about. She was burning with curiosity for the dance to be over, when she could seek Corabel and question her. But the dance was not over yet, and it seemed to her the most interminable she had ever known. She longed to clap her hands and make the music cease; but even Freda, at S——, did not quite like to do that in a public ball-room, and she had to wait like other people till the musicians themselves chose to let their sweet liveliness come to a conclusion in those die-away sounds that have so often stopped flying feet and grieved bounding hearts.

"At last!" cried Freda, as the music ceased.

"Alas!" replied her partner, and Freda laughed her saucy laugh.

"I want to speak to my friend, Miss Bell," she said imperiously; "take me to her."

And he took her. Corabel still leant on her partner's arm, standing before one of the pillars that supported the domed roof; but, as Freda came up to them, the stranger gently withdrew his arm, made a civil bow, and walked away.

"He avoids me," thought Freda, with a rapid pain stabbing her heart as she thought it. "He actually hates me." Then with a slight bend she dismissed her own partner, and turned eagerly to her friend. "Well?" she cried eagerly.

"Well?" answered Corabel, cool and un-excited.

"How did it come about? Who intro-duced you?"

"Oh, to him, you mean?"

"Of course, I mean to him."

"He asked to be introduced to me, Freda. He asked General Gray."

"He did, did he?"

"Yes. It was rather pleasant, wasn't it? I feel flattered."

"And who is he? and how does he talk?"

"I don't know who he is; I didn't catch the name; but he talks delightfully, and unlike other people. He is one of the most agreeable men I ever met—but original, decidedly original."

"*But* original," cried Freda, with a disdainful emphasis on her friend's word; "what are they worth if they're not original? Nothing!"

Corabel smiled. "He is worth something then," she said calmly.

"But, Corabel, what made him ask to be introduced to you? I'm not rude. You're as nice as ever you can be; but why, specially, did *he* want an introduction?"

"Ah, that I can't tell you; but he took a little trouble about it, really he did, Freda. I was in the refreshment-room eating an ice, when they came up together, and I saw him touch General Gray's arm, and say what sounded like, 'That is the lady;' and then the General brought him straight up to me and said, 'Here is a gentleman wishes to be introduced to you, Miss Bell;' and then he murmured his name, as they always do, you know, so that I couldn't hear it ; and so we danced together, and that's all, I suppose, Freda."

" No, indeed, it isn't all. What did you talk about ?"

" Oh, what did we talk about ? About a good many things ; not much of ordinary ball-room talk, that does not seem in his line, but about this place a little, and about Jamaica, and then some word made us both think of a passage in George Eliot at the same minute, and so we spoke about books."

" About books ?" cried Freda discontentedly. " Nobody ever talks to me about books ; and yet you know, Corabel, I have read lots and lots."

" Yes, and very good books too, not only idle ones," laughed Corabel ; " and so I told him."

" You told him ?" cried she, almost breathless.

"Yes; he was surprised at my quoting something from Macaulay, and when he said a few words, my recognising Sydney Smith in them; and he remarked I was a great reader. So I told him that I and the friend I lived with read together every morning. And then he asked if my friend was *chaperoning* me—he thought you were some respectable wall-flower, Freda—and I said yes, should I show her to him? and I showed him—you."

"And then what did he say?"

"Shall I tell you?"

"Certainly. By all means, tell me."

"You are sure you won't mind it?"

"Tell me, and see."

"He said he should not have thought that you were a reader."

"Oh—h," with a very great prolongation; "he said that, did he?"

CHAPTER X.

A MOONLIGHT FLITTING.

THE two girls met at rather a late breakfast next morning. Freda was silent, and looked a little pale ; Corabel, who never had much colour, appeared as usual, but regarded her friend with rather anxious eyes.

"I wonder whether you are strong, Freda," she said. "You do everything, and your spirits and energy are indubitable, but I wonder whether you have ever got quite strong since your illness. People who look as you do—so radiant, and with such brilliant colouring—are very often indeed not strong."

And a sad expression passed over Corabel's face as the idea of Freda in failing health and strength presented itself, against her will, to her mind. But Freda only laughed at the idea with all her usual gaiety.

"Strong," she cried, " I am as strong as a bird—as a lark. What could put such a notion as that into your head ?"

"You are tired with the ball, at any rate, and must give yourself some rest."

"Oh yes, I am tired with the ball, because it was the most tiresome ball I ever was at in my life. It was a *horrid* ball—was not it, Corabel ?"

"No; was it ?" answered the other, surprised. "I did not know it; it seemed to me much like other balls. I never care for them as you do, you know, Freda; but I thought this one rather pleasanter than usual."

" I dare say you did," said Freda, almost spitefully, " because you flirted at it."

" I flirted ! And whom did I flirt with, I wonder ?"

" With the stranger, of course !"

" Well, that *is* nonsense. I danced one

dance with him, and we talked about books, and all those sort of things."

" As if people couldn't flirt about books."

Corabel laughed.

" Well, *we* did not, at any rate; nothing could be less like flirting than the little conversation we had, and he stayed a very short time with me, after the dance was over, and did not pay me the least attention."

" He asked to be introduced to you."

" Yes, he did ; but that is not flirting."

" It's the way to flirting, if it is not the thing itself." Then Freda looked very earnestly into Corabel's face, and suddenly said, " Why did you say you were a widow at heart ?"

" I didn't say so," cried Corabel, startled.

" Yes you did, or something of the sort, and I want to know—I want to understand—oh ! Corabel, you are not married too ?"

" No, Freda," replied she, half laughing ; " I am certainly not married."

" Then why are you a widow at heart, Corabel ? For you are one, whether you called yourself one or not. You are not

like a girl; you don't care for balls and things
as girls do; you are like a person who has
been happily married in a quiet sort of a way
for ten years, and been keeping house all the
time."

"And is that being a widow at heart,
Freda?" cried Corabel, and she laughed out-
right now.

"You know what I mean," replied Freda
pettishly, "it's not being a girl; and if you
are quiet and subdued like that when you
are a girl, and *haven't* got a husband, you
must be like a widow. Corabel, when you said
I was your chaperon, did he know I was a
widow or think I was married?"

"He! When I said you were my chaperon? Oh, you mean my partner last
night. He was surprised, and asked if your
husband was there; and I said you were a
widow."

"And what did he say then?" cried Freda
with eagerness.

"He laughed, and remarked that you
would not be one long."

"He is an intolerable ruffian," cried Freda
with flushed cheeks. "I never hated a man

so much in my life, and that is saying a good deal."

" Yes," replied Corabel quietly, " that *is* saying a good deal."

" But about you," persisted Freda, " what makes you like what you are ? I could understand at Clapham, when you had to teach, and it wasn't nice ; but now—why are you so now, Corabel ? Are not you happy ?"

There was a wistful look in Freda's splendid eyes, and a tone of regret in her voice, which touched Corabel. She got up and kissed her.

" Yes, I am very happy, dear," she cried ; " you make me very happy."

Freda returned the kiss warmly, and then there was a little pause.

" I will tell you how it is," said Corabel presently—" just once I will tell you, Freda, and then we will not talk of it ever again. I did love some one, and he loved me, but we did not marry ; it is all over, and I am content now — but — it makes a *difference*, Freda."

" Oh, Corabel, how strange — how very strange ! What an odd, *odd* thing it is to love! and for that to alter the world and one's life for ever—I can't understand it— I never could understand it. What is it? How is it? How does it come? What is it like? I wonder—I wonder—shall I ever know?"

Corabel looked at the beautiful creature, as she stood before her, with sparkling eyes, rose-tinted cheeks, and innocent child-face.

"Yes, Freda," she said, almost solemnly, " you will know some day; and I hope you will then be very happy—happier than you have any idea of now."

" Maud had wanted to marry some one, and Letty married Jack, and thought of nobody else; and now here are you—everybody appears to be in love but me. It's really too bad—it seems a shame; and if it *is* so nice I ought to have it, because I always do get the best of everything."

" Have patience, and it will come to you all in good time."

"I hope it will be before I'm old—quite old, and don't care about it," said Freda rather gravely. " And now, Corabel, do let us go out and take a walk. It will shake us up, and do us good. I really feel as if I wanted to be shaken up and done good to this morning. Sometimes I think I should like to be a missionary."

" A missionary !" cried Corabel, sure that her ears had deceived her, and that she had not heard the word aright.

" Yes, a missionary," replied Freda quite calmly ; " it would be a change, and I should make a good one. I can always get people to do what I want, which is the chief thing ; and it would be an out-of-door life ; and it would be amusing making them wear clothes and seeing how awkward they were in them ; and I could dress them up just as I like, and they not know. I should dress all the men as bishops and swell coachmen—those are the two best dresses; and it would be nice to have a lot of bishops and coachmen mixed up to-gether—wouldn't it, Corabel ? And then all the time I should be doing the greatest pos-sible good that any one can do, and I should be of real use ! And sometimes I do almost think I should like to do good and be of use. How odd it must be to feel you are a good example. I wonder whether I should like to be a good example. I think I might for a very short time, just at first."

And so the two friends went out on the esplanade together.

" I am thinking of asking my Vicar and his sister here," said Freda presently.

Corabel was silent for a minute, and then replied :

" Do you suppose they would like this sort of place ?—a watering-place. I hardly fancy it would suit them."

"Oh, I don't think they would mind. I would ask them directly if he hadn't wanted me to marry him. I couldn't do it when he asked me, because I was married already ; but if he asked me now I could, so it would be rather awkward. I told you he wanted me to marry him, didn't I, Corabel?"

" Yes, Freda, you told me he wanted you to marry him."

" And I had a very good excuse then for not doing it, because I was married already ; but I have none now."

" Then perhaps you had better do it."

" No, I am quite sure I had better not," replied Freda very earnestly. " I did not like being married at all, and I am quite determined never to marry again unless I am in love."

"That is a very good resolution," said a voice behind them.

It was a low voice, and it mixed itself with the winds and the waves, but it *was* a voice ; and both the girls distinguished the words, and looked over their shoulders at the same moment.

They looked in vain, however, for they saw no one. They had left the esplanade for the shore, which, at this part, was fine, bold, and rocky, and some high rocks were behind them.

"There !" cried Freda ; "this is supernatural ! Did *you* hear it ?"

"Yes, I heard it."

"And yet it can't have been a real voice—not a human voice, at least—for there is no one."

"But it must have been a real human voice, since we both heard it."

"What nonsense, Corabel! If one can hear what isn't, why shouldn't two ?"

"But if one heard what isn't, it would be

because her nerves were in some queer peculiar state which made her do so."

"And if one had her nerves in that queer peculiar state, why shouldn't two?"

"Only that it would be so very unlikely that it is just the same as impossible."

"Do you think that's either logic or argument? I affirm that if one can hear a thing that doesn't exist, it is more likely that two should, than not. Grant that one can, and the rest follows. If no one died, no one could; but if one does, then it becomes easy and natural that two should also."

At that moment a gentleman, tall and active, passed rather hastily by them, stepping lightly and rapidly from rock to rock; he turned his head towards them as he did so, and lifted his hat, to which salutation Corabel replied by a bow. Freda stared at him astonished, and then walked on, throwing her head a little more backward than usual, as if to mark the fact that she had not bowed at all.

It was the stranger, who had excited her interest so much on the previous evening, and who had danced with her friend.

"Well, if it was he spoke—if he was listening—the mean thing!—and answered—impudent wretch!—it's intolerable—it's frightful! I've known a man hanged for less than that—haven't you, Corabel?" cried Freda, her face all aflame, and her indignation, whether feigned or real, immense.

"You've known a man hanged! what things you do say, Freda," laughed Corabel. "No, I never knew a man hanged at all, nor did you."

"We ought then; the law is all wrong as usual. Men ought to be hanged for social crimes more than for murder."

"Isn't murder a social crime?"

"Yes, if you call murdering a form of society—like dancing—but I don't; and I don't think it is; but listening is a social crime, and so is impudence, and men should be hanged for them, if for anything."

"I don't think that is a mean man," said Corabel.

"I wish he had never been born," cried Freda, and she spoke as if she really meant it; but then she talked all her wild nonsense in that manner. Mr. Underwood was not the only hearer of Freda's words who had doubted whether she was full of quaint humour, or almost an idiot. "What business had he to be born without asking me? What right had he to intrude into the world without first ascertaining whether the world wanted him?"

"I can't say about the world," answered her friend, "but there is a very good reason for his not having asked *you*, for I don't think you were born yourself till he was at least eight or nine years old."

"Such a horrid age!" cried she, quite as if that was his fault too. "What a nuisance he must have been just when I was born—boys of eight or nine are unbearable."

"And are babies better?"

"He must have been a *dreadful* baby. Babies are delightful, but he must have been a shocking one. Seriously, I don't believe he ever can have been a baby at all; I think he came at first, a big bad boy, and only went on growing till he was a big bad man."

That night Freda was restless and found sleep difficult. She sprang from her bed between three and four o'clock in the morning, and looked out of her window on to the sea. A large full moon hung in the sky and cast its exquisite light over the blue expanse of water which lay there without a single ripple on its breast, over the heavens, not calmer or more pure, and over the earth. But the unmistakable moonlight, which is called silvery for want of a better name, and which is really unlike anything else in the world, was becoming mixed with another light, that radiant twilight which, on midsummer mornings, precedes the rising of the sun. The two lights, distinct yet mingling, and both shining together, were strangely beautiful, and almost took Freda's breath away with delight.

"Is it possible?" she whispered, for she would not have spoken aloud for the world; "both together? Oh, who could ever have thought it! Oh, how I love you for coming just now—just when I happened to look out of window! How kind everything is!"

She dressed herself hastily, never taking her eyes off sky and sea while she put on her clothes, and then ran gleefully out of doors, grudging keenly the few moments of time when in passage and staircase she lost the lovely sight that the sun and the moon had graciously prepared for her. When she was really out of doors, with all these beauties entirely her own, she raised her eyes quite devoutly above her head, clapped her pretty hands together, and said with great simplicity, " Thank God."

For some time she was content to stand just where she was, and only look at the sea and the sky. But Freda was ambitious in all things. She was not contented with the good : she coveted the perfect. And it suddenly struck her that perfection could only be obtained from the top of a cliff that rose abruptly at one end of the esplanade, and to the top of which she had never yet climbed. The height was not great, and there was an easy way up ; and she thought that to ascend it now would be delicious. It was very little more than three o'clock. The whole world that she saw before and around her was hers alone ; the very sky was hers ; she was the only living creature left on earth everybody else was asleep. She might have been the last woman, the only being remaining with life and animation, of all the countless millions that had inhabited this orb. "Oh, if some day, when all have died out, one must be last and alone," thought Freda, "I should like to be that one;" and then she added her favourite phrase—"just for a little while."

She walked and ran, and ran and walked, by turns, till she actually found herself on the top of the cliff. Then she threw herself down on the grass, and after blowing a few grateful kisses up to the sky, looked round her, and was for a time in perfect bliss.

The cliff was a sort of promontory, and the sea lay in front of her and on each side of her. The moon still hung large and round in the heavens, and still poured her silvery radiance on the ocean, but its lustre perceptibly diminished, while the splendid colours of sunrise were filling the eastern sky with incredible glory.

"Certainly," cried Freda with conviction, "it did require God to make *this!*"

It was not only the infinite beauty, it was that peculiar freshness and purity that only is felt in early morning air before the world has waked up to pollute it. It was God's world she was for a moment inhabiting, not man's.

She lay there quite quiet and quite happy for a long time, with no conscious thoughts—no thoughts put into mere human words—but thinking none the less on that account. I suppose our best and highest thoughts are always those for which we cannot find words. The world has not existed long enough—there has not been time yet, for man to make words for everything—and there *are* thoughts and feelings which probably will never find definite expression in time at all; for that we must wait for eternity.

But after awhile our Freda grew tired of being quiet, and wanted to play again, so she sprang to her feet and glanced about her, just to see what was the happiest thing she could do next. She looked straight before her—as her graceful swaying figure stood, itself making a charming landmark—on the cliff, and there she saw the boundless expanse of blue sea. She looked to the right, that was where she had come from, and there was sea also; but before the eye reached the sea, the village of S------ with its pretty church and fair terraces of houses arrested it very pleasantly. And then she looked to the left. There again was sea, for, as I have before said, the cliff she stood on was a sort of promontory, stretching out with water on three sides of it ; but the sea to the left was the most distant of all the sea. And running down to it was a sweet little green valley, full of trees and flowers ; and nestled therein was a charming thatched house, all over shining climbing things, and with smooth lawn and well-kept gardens sloping down to the very shore—to the very blue ocean itself. It was all on a miniature scale—valley, house, and garden — but in its very smallness lay its delight.

Freda gave a little cry of pleasure, and ran rapidly down the zigzag walk that led from the top of the cliff to this fairy paradise.

"I shall steal some flowers," she cried, enchanted. "I never did steal anything. It would be heavenly to steal flowers—flowers !— in the first sweet dawn of a summer morning. All alone, running down to a strange house to steal. I shall understand how house-breakers feel. I shall like that ; but pickpocketing must be nicest. It must be deliciously exciting to put your hand into a pocket without the *least* idea what it may bring out of it—a flimsy handkerchief with a hole in it, a useless bunch of keys, or a purse with a hundred-pound note at each end. I do think I should like to be a pickpocket."

Here she stopped on the side of the hill and laughed brightly, with a sweet ringing sound in the laughter, which made her put her hand over her mouth and say, " Hush ! they don't make a noise when they are stealing." And so she went the rest of the way on tip-toe, though it is very inconvenient to descend a steep hill on the tips of your toes. This novel method of progress delayed her a little, but she was charmed to find herself in the garden at last, alone with the flowers. It was a pretty garden, nicely kept, and full of bright blossoms.

" Let us be conscientious," said Freda with solemnity, and she gathered a rose here and a geranium there, and a heliotrope here again, so as not to injure the effect of all the shining colours. " It's not that I'm trying not to be found out, it's only that I'm conscientious, and wouldn't on any account spoil the pretty garden. I like to be conscientious when I steal."

She played with the radiant blossoms before she plucked them, making the very most of her pleasure.

"What a pity it is things must come to an end," she said softly, with a little sigh. "I should like to be stealing flowers all day."

"Would you indeed?" said a man's voice behind her.

She gave a musical scream, and turned hastily round, her hands full of flowers, her hat falling off at the back of her head, her eyes shining with the delight she had felt, her lips half pouting, half smiling, and showing small pearly teeth between them. What a picture she would have made! the purity of the sweet complexion only yielding to that of the transparent eyes and childlike face.

She quite started back and almost dropped her flowers when she saw it was the stranger who had accosted her.

"Why he haunts me," she said to herself. "I do hope he is going to haunt me."

Then she spoke aloud, instantly seizing on the advantage he had given her.

"Are you listening again?" she said sweetly. "How mean!"

"Listening, and mean? What are you thinking of?" he replied severely. "It is you——"

"Didn't you do it on the shore yesterday? Answer me that. Was it not you who said it was a very good resolution?"

"And what if it was?" he asked, rather startled.

"Only that was like a spy, and so is this. Listening and looking—it *is* mean, isn't it?"

She spoke in the pleasantest manner, with the most attractive smile, and the last question was put as if she really wanted to know.

"And what do you think of coming here and stealing my flowers in the middle of the night?" he began.

"Oh, the middle of the night!" she cried, waving the little hand that did not hold the flowers at the sky. "For shame! look there, is *that* the middle of the night? Is it really all wasted upon you?"

He took no notice of her speech or her

movement, or even of the glories in the sky, but answered her gravely and morosely.

" It is not four o'clock, or at least it is very little more than four o'clock. You have no business to come here and take what does not belong to you. These flowers are mine. You are as much a thief as any poor person who steals. It is not respectable for a girl like you to be running about at this hour by yourself."

At these words Freda's gay laugh rang forth.

" Oh, I am glad you said that," she cried, really delighted. " I'm not respectable ! Respectable ! Now do you really suppose I ever thought I *was* respectable ?"

And she laughed again with the pleasure of a child.

" I don't know," he replied, " whether you will like to have the police sent for."

She looked at him rather eagerly.

" Well, I don't know either," she said. " I don't quite know, but I rather think I should. It would be a novelty, at any rate, and it might be a little nice. What do *you* think ?" she added confidentially. " What

view do you take of it, now ? I dare say
you're a man of the world, and I might be
guided by your opinion."

Again she looked in his face sweetly and
inquiringly, with the utmost difficulty pre-
serving her gravity, but still she did preserve
it.

I don't know whether he had as much
difficulty in keeping grave and treating her
as he did, but not a muscle of his face relaxed
as he fixed a pair of very bright and handsome
brown eyes upon her.

" I suppose you are married, since you live
there ?" was her next question, nodding at
the house as she spoke.

He answered her question by another.

" Are you going to walk back to S—— by
yourself, just when all the labourers and
fishermen will be about ?"

" I suppose not," she replied demurely. " I
suppose I shall be escorted by—the police." ·

" I shall walk with you," he said ; " but
what are you or your friend either thinking
of, that you run about the country in this
way, and at any hour ? It is very wrong—it
is very wrong indeed."

"My friend is blameless," cried she, "so you needn't mind. It is *she* you asked to be introduced to, you know. Come back with me and breakfast with us, and then you can tell her what a disreputable pair you think us."

"She seems good and sensible, and *you* have had trials. You might both know better."

"How do you know I have had trials? What do you mean by trials?"

He bit his lips, looked hard at her, and paused before he replied.

Then he said, with some hesitation : "So young a lady—who is still wearing mourning for—who is——"

Here he stopped, and seemed unable to finish his speech. The colour rose into Freda's cheeks, and, to her own astonishment, the tears into her eyes. She had not an idea why the words affected her thus, or why her tears came at an allusion to that which, when it happened, had caused her no grief.

The stranger looked at her very earnestly, and as he saw her emotion his own face became scarlet. He turned abruptly round and walked a few paces away from her. He thought he heard the sound of her voice recalling him. At any rate, he came back.

" Come," he said, " we had better return to S——, had we not ?"

" And leave this *pretty* place ?" she cried, looking regretfully round at the flowers and trees. " What a hurry you're in. I could stay here for ever."

" You had better not stay till the servants and people are up and about; you had better come over the hill at once. I will see you home."

" I am glad I came here," she cried. " I had not the slightest idea I should meet you. I did not know you lived here. I had never seen or heard of this place, never. I had never before been unable to sleep, and looked out to see moonlight and sunrise mingle in irresistible beauty; nor did I ever leave the house at this wondrous hour, or climb this particular cliff, and from its height find a lovely valley full of flowers ; and oh ! never in my whole life before did I long for the pleasure of stealing, and of stealing flowers! Why could it be? What does it mean?"

" It was fate !" he answered, and she did not know whether his voice was indeed solemn and sad, or whether, like her, he was playing with life. But was she playing? was all she had just said mere play? That she did not know, either.

A strong desire to remain longer in this lovely place, and enjoy the delights of flowers and shrubs blooming at the very edge of the blue ocean, seized upon Freda. And why should this tyrannical man take her away? It was she who was always despot, and reigned imperiously over the wills of those who came near her. Was she going to abdicate her throne now, and give her sceptre up to this stranger?

" Couldn't you go into the house—your own house, and remain there for an hour?" she said persuasively; "and after that we might walk home to breakfast."

" And you ?" he asked, surprised.

" Oh, I want to stay here among the flowers—looking *through* flowers at the sea— till daylight has become a settled thing, and there is no more varying twilight—and I am sure you would like to go indoors for a bit; now, wouldn't you?"

He could not help smiling, and it was the first smile he had given to her quaint humours. But though he smiled he shook his head.

"Not to-day," he replied; and it seemed almost as if he was speaking to a child he wished at once to subdue and to please; "not to-day. You shall come another day, and stay here as long as you like; but just now you must let me walk home with you."

Freda gave him a glance of saucy defiance —defeated, yet still determined.

"We shall see about *that*," she cried, with gay resolve; and the next minute she ran from him and began scaling the cliff where it touched the garden—at by no means as easy a part to ascend as that by which she had descended, where there was a kind of path. But Freda was indifferent to these sort of difficulties, and she ran up the side of the cliff like a goat.

He looked after her retreating form with admiration and disapprobation, and for a moment remained doubtful whether he should follow her. Then he turned suddenly, and took another way, hidden by trees, of which she knew nothing, but by which he was aware he could intercept her steps before she reached the top of the hill.

She ran up without stopping to draw breath; then she glanced over her shoulder furtively, to see what he was about, and stopped short, dismayed, when she found he had disappeared from her sight.

"He has actually gone into the house," she cried—"actually!"

A dull, blank sense of disappointment came over her: this disappointment was not for herself, but about him. It was not because she had lost her amusement and was to be deprived of the pleasure of his society, but because she thought his conduct low and stupid, and not what she would have expected his conduct would be.

"He is a poltroon," she said; "he has quietly yielded. He said he would walk home with me — and I have conquered; he is a poltroon."

As a general thing, she liked to conquer

and have her own way, and preferred the
people who gave up to her. Now her feelings were quite inconsistent with those that
had hitherto been natural to her; she felt
aggrieved and depressed that her own way
was given her without a word, and that her
opponent had quietly yielded the field. She
had asked him to go into the house—his own
house—and he had gone; she had declared
she would walk back by herself, and he
permitted her to do so. Very well, then she
would not think of him. She would not
trouble herself about him any more. She
would go home to Corabel and breakfast,
and trust that her path and his might never
again cross each other. And so after standing still for a minute and looking rather
pitifully back at the flowers and the trees,
the pretty thatched house, and the blue sea
that lay in front of them, she turned again,
faced the hill, and then ran hastily up
it. She came, as she did so, on a sort
of sheep-walk, which went on a nearly
level line round the shoulder of the cliff.
She went breathlessly on, turned the corner,
ran up against a man who was approaching

to meet her, caught her foot on a stone, stumbled, fell, and would have rolled down the grassy slope into the foaming sea some hundreds of feet below, if she had not been caught before she reached the ground, raised, and forcibly held, clasped in the arms of the stranger.

CHAPTER XI.

HER FIRST MARRIAGE.

E looked at her for one moment, as he held her there, and a cloud of strange conflicting emotions passed over his face. You would have felt an awe and a wonder as to what he was feeling, or what he might do next. A man with that face might be a murderer, or might be a martyr just for a minute. Then the storm of passion was gone, and he was once more calm and impassive.

"Take care," he said coolly; "that heedless step would have been your death-step if I had not been here to catch you. I know that sharp corner, and most dangerous it is."

And then he let her go.

She remained quite still and subdued, trembling a little. How beautiful she looked as she stood there—her radiant face almost pale, her eyes shining softly, her lips slightly parted. A yearning regretful expression came slowly into her face, and she trembled a little more.

" I don't want to die," she said in a whisper.

" You are not going to die yet," he answered her; but his manner was not as rough as his words.

" You saved me," she said, still speaking like a whisper.

" Yes," he answered, with a short laugh, " I saved you—what for ?"

The last two words did not appear to be addressed to her, or to himself, but to some listener in space, who might be able to answer them, as assuredly neither she nor he could have done.

" If I had died !" she cried nervously. "Ah ! where should I be now ? I don't wish it—I shouldn't like it—would you ? Would you wish to die ?"

She questioned earnestly as one who greatly

desired an honest answer, and fixed her brilliant piercing eyes on his.

Her manner compelled a reply serious and sincere. He reflected.

"No," he said slowly; "life has not much wherewith to commend itself to me, but I *don't* wish to die—does any one?"

"Benjamin does," said Freda softly, "and he wants me to go with him; only I have begged him not, and he has promised."

"Benjamin!" cried the stranger; "who is Benjamin?"

"He is a little, little dying boy, like an angel, who loves me very dearly," said Freda. She was subdued, and spoke with seriousness. "But he is sure of heaven, while I—but I *couldn't* go anywhere else—could I?" And she fixed her eager eyes once more on his.

It seemed to her that he turned a little pale as she did so.

"How can I tell?" he answered her gloomily. "You know yourself, and your thoughts, and your wishes. Why do you ask me? Is there any one on earth I know less than I do you? It is not your beauty that will save you, nor your sweet ways, your gay words and innocent laughter —*that* I can tell you. Can I tell anything more ?"

Freda, however, was already recovering from the shock and its effects on her nerves, and his words, though not very consolatory, did not affect her as they would have done a few minutes sooner. Her spirits were elastic, and rose easily, almost eagerly.

The stranger walked home with her.

"Will you tell me your name ?" she said ; "it is stupid always calling you the stranger."

She spoke as if it was his fault, and he suppressed a smile, while he answered :

"I did not know you called me the stranger, or anything else. My name is Percival."

"How can we speak of you without calling you something ?" she asked simply.

"Very true, but I did not know you spoke of me."

"We do, though. And I shall have a great triumph over Corabel for this adventure."

"Do you talk to all men as you do to me?" he asked abruptly, as if he could not help it; then coloured, bit his lips, and looked vexed.

But she did not notice his embarrassment. The question seemed to her quite natural, and she gave it a straightforward answer.

"No, I don't. I dislike most men, and the rest are tiresome—except one clergyman. I am very fond, indeed, of one clergyman."

"And he is——" He looked keenly at her.

"Ah, you wouldn't know if I told you—what is the use of telling you? But I *think* I am going to ask him here, and then you will meet him. He is the best man I know —the best man I ever knew. I would ask him directly if I was quite sure he wouldn't be in the way."

"That is paying a great compliment to the best man you ever knew."

"I never pay compliments—I don't like them—they are silly. Don't you think so? But you don't understand about Mr. Underwood; there are reasons. I know what I am talking about, but you don't."

" The name of the best man is Underwood, then ?"

" You talk of him as if he were at a wedding. Yes, his name is Underwood. I have not seen him—oh, for so long a time. I should like to see him ; and I think Corabel would like him very much. I wonder whether you would. Do you like men ?"

" That is rather a general question. I like some men."

" As a rule *I* dislike them, but sometimes men like each other **very** *very* much. *They* did—it was astonishing. I could not understand it."

" They ? I beg your pardon—who are you speaking of ?"

Freda stared at him, and then blushed a lovely rosy red that spread all over her fair face.

" Oh, I was not attending," she cried ; " I was thinking aloud. I did not mean to say that—never mind."

" Would your good clergyman approve of your stealing flowers ?"

" Oh, but you know," said Freda, sidling nearer to him and speaking almost penitently, " that was a joke. I wouldn't really steal—of course I would not. I was only playing at it, because I was up so early."

"But you *took* the flowers," he persisted, " and they were not yours. Where is the difference ? What makes it play, or earnest ?"

Freda looked a little puzzled.

"But I *couldn't,* you know," she said ; " it's not possible. I couldn't be a thief. It's one of the commandments. I couldn't break a commandment. It was just play. Here, take the flowers. I won't keep them a moment if you are going to be so very disagreeable about them as that."

She turned to him with a playful movement, and in the gentlest, most refined manner possible, with a little laugh and a deprecating, almost coaxing glance, threw the scented blossoms in his face.

He caught them as they fell, and gave them back to her—all but one spray of myrtle in full flower, which he kept himself.

" Here, take them," he cried; " I give them to you. They are mine, so you may fairly take them."

Freda caught them eagerly with both her hands, buried her face in them for a moment, and dropped some light kisses among them.

" Pretty dears," she cried, and softly caressed them.

When they had reached her house, she desired him to come in and have some breakfast; but he positively declined, and was not to be persuaded.

" I will call later in the day if you will allow me," he said, " and shall hope to find you no worse for your exertions."

Freda wished him a gay good-morning, and then rushed laughing upstairs.

Meantime Mr. Percival rapidly retraced his steps homewards—with knit brows and fiercely-compressed lips—plunged in thoughts the nature of which his dearest friend would have found it very difficult to guess from his face.

Mr. Percival did call, according to his promise, on that afternoon; and this visit was the first of many others. The three young people, to use a popular phrase, " took to each other." The girls were encouraging, and the man was willing. An acquaintanceship under such circumstances speedily glides into intimacy.

Freda was interested, pleased, delighted. A change came gradually over her. She was softened; she was almost subdued; she acquired a habit of blushing, and another of listening instead of talking. A sweet, tender light stole into her eyes; she smiled oftener, and laughed less frequently.

Mr. Percival's attentions were, perhaps, more openly offered to Corabel than to Freda. He spoke more to the elder of the two ladies, and had a trick of seeming to consider that she was the mistress of the house, to whom respect was to be paid, instead of the other. He often found fault with Freda, never with Corabel; he disputed with the first, and agreed with the second; and yet Freda was not discontented, for she believed he felt a friendship for her, as she could not but be aware that she was an object of interest to him, and that whoever else he might be speaking to, he was never unconscious of her presence. Thus *her* interest in him, which seemed to have been first excited by the want of any corresponding feeling on

his part, was now increased by its existence.

Corabel liked their new friend much, in her
sedate manner, and took real pleasure in his
society. Sometimes the idea crossed her
mind, that he and Freda might grow to care
for each other with a feeling that was more
than friendship. But Freda in love, subdued,
captive to the will of another, seemed impossible ; nor could she detect anything that
caused more than a momentary suspicion
of a warmer feeling than friendship on the
part of Freda's rather stern judge, Mr.
Percival.

One day he had called and found Corabel
alone. Their conversation turned first on
books, as usual with them, but glided off to
other things ; and, in answer to some remark
of his, Corabel expressed a little envy of his
lonely retirement, from which he need not
seek the more bustling atmosphere of S——,
unless he liked.

"I am quite happy here," she said; "and
am really enjoying it. But I am glad that
watering-places have a season, and that Mrs.
Fane will not care to stay when the season is

past. Watering-place life, *for* life, would be indescribably tiresome."

" I can well believe you would find it so," he replied, with an air of conviction, adding, as if he was only speaking the most common-place truism : " But for a pretty, heartless woman, like Mrs. Fane, it must be life itself."

Corabel was startled, and a little indignant. " Heartless !" she exclaimed ; " Freda heart-less ! Why, there is not a warmer-hearted creature in the world than Mrs. Fane, or one who is more above any frivolous kind of existence. Do you really misjudge her so much ? you who know her almost well !"

He looked very steadily at her, paused, re-flected, and then replied :

" I do not underrate her intellect," he said. " Notwithstanding the wild nonsense she talks, I see that she is clever, and that she plays with her own mind and thoughts, as she does with those of other people. But warm-hearted—is that really the case ? I should have thought her, if as pure and transparent as ice, at least as cold also."

" No, no," cried Corabel ; " she has great

capability of loving, and even of unselfishness and self-devotion. She is full of sweet, bright impulses. She requires only training. Examine, for example, our relations to each other. Her kindness to me is boundless; but it takes so completely the form of affection that I do not believe she has the least idea that I ought to, or do, feel gratitude for her."

" I dare say," he said, with the politeness of feeling, " that she knows she has at least as much to be grateful to you for. However, I must confess that you are giving me a surprisingly new view of Mrs. Fane's character. When I called her heartless, I thought I was using a word that no one could for a moment dispute described her. You must allow, Miss Bell, that when one sees a mere girl so very gay, so short a time after her husband's death, it does not look as if she had much heart; now, does it ?"

Corabel's face clouded over, and she sighed.

" Mr. Fane has been dead more than a year," she replied ; " but all marriages are not happy ones, Mr. Percival. You see, Mrs. Fane is scarcely more than a child now, yet

she has been a widow for a year. Don't you
think it likely that as she was a child when
she married him, she may have become his
wife more from obedience to others than by
her own wish."

"Miserable mistake!" he cried. "And
he, did he care for her? Did you know Mr.
Fane?"

"No. I never knew Mrs. Fane till he had
gone abroad. They were not together when
I first knew her, and he died soon afterwards.
I never saw him."

"And only know him through her report?"

"Not quite," replied Corabel. "I had
heard of him years ago, before I, or he either,
knew of Freda's existence."

"Indeed!" cried Mr. Percival; and he
looked surprised, though it would have been
difficult to say why he should look surprised
at Miss Bell having heard of Mr. Fane. Perhaps it was merely because politeness de-
manded he should show some emotion, and
he thought surprise as good a one to assume
as any other. He did not say more than this
"indeed" for a moment, and then, with re-
stored calmness of manner, added: "And I

suppose you never heard any good of the poor man, since he could not win his wife's affections."

"Yes, I heard a great deal of good of him then. I never heard anything but good of him till I knew Freda. Their characters did not suit, and I fancy his temper was bad. He did not understand her, I'm sure, or make allowance for her wild gaiety and childishness. She thinks he did not love her. But that is impossible, for why else should he have married her?"

"Why, indeed?" replied Mr. Percival gravely.

"I suppose he fell in love, as it is called," continued Corabel, with a touch of gentle scorn in her voice, "with her wonderful beauty; a worthless sort of love, Mr. Percival, and a selfish one—a love that demands much and yields little, and from which patience and forbearance cannot spring. He must have loved her, but he did not love her enough."

"Or he loved her too much," cried he. "Only a daring man would trust his happiness in such hands as hers."

"Now what does this mean?" thought

Corabel, interested yet perplexed. " Is he falling in love with her himself, and is all this to sound and try me ?   What does it mean ?" She could not answer the questions to her own satisfaction.

" A man who loved her enough," she said calmly, " would have thought more of her and less of himself.   As to loving too much, I don't know what that means, unless it is foolish indulgence, and I am quite sure Mr. Fane was not too indulgent.   I am quite sure he was not indulgent enough.   A man has no business to expect, what he does not marry, instead of what he does.   Mr. Fane married a beautiful child, and, if he did not treat her as such, his unhappiness was his own fault ; and, what is worse, her unhappiness was his fault also."

" He expiated that fault pretty soon though," said Mr. Percival, rather bitterly. " Her unhappiness has not troubled her much.   He made her perfectly happy by his death."

" You seem to be angry at her gay spirits ! As if a child like Freda could be made miserable, even at the time, or could suffer a year afterwards, for the loss of a husband who did not suit her, and was not kind to her."

" *Was* he not kind to her ?"

" You think that impossible ; and so it seems. But I fancy it was so. He was harsh and stern, which is the same thing as unkindness to a gay child."

" Well," said Mr. Percival, rising to take his leave, " I dare say you are right. I know nothing about it, but you will forgive my curiosity ; it is impossible not to feel—interested, in your friend."

" How strange men are," thought Corabel, when he had left her alone ; " I am sure he is falling in love with Freda. Nothing else would account for his asking and thinking so much about her first marriage ; and yet he feels so differently from what I should have expected. He appears sorry that she did not care for her husband, and is not unhappy in his loss ; yet surely if a man wants to marry a widow, he would rather she had not been so very much in love with her first husband, or so very happy in her first marriage. Men always *do* feel differently from what one would expect. I suppose a young widow, being gay and full of spirits like my poor Freda, does not accord with his ideal, and he would rather sacrifice her happiness, and even give up winning her first affections, than have his ideal interfered with. That is the only way I can account for it. Men always *are* odd."

While Corabel mused about him in the pretty morning-room facing the sea, Mr. Percival, plunged in deep and apparently unpleasant reflections, was walking rapidly away from it. His hat was pulled down over his brows, his hands thrust deep into his pockets, and almost as if he did not know in which direction he was going, he threaded his way among the back streets of S——, instead of taking one of the frequented walks near the sea. While he was still in the town, he was overtaken by a heavy shower of rain, mixed with hail, and he stood up under a projection over the door of a mean little house for shelter. He leant against the door, and it gave way as he did so. Taking the hint, he entered the cottage, and was amazed at the scene that instantly presented itself to his eyes.

A bed faced the door, and in it lay a sick child, with a thin face, whiter than the pillows that supported his head, though pillow and bedding were all not only scrupulously clean, but of fine linen and good materials, by no means in character with the rest of the apartment. By the bed knelt Freda, her hat on the ground at her side, and her sweet face smiling at the sick child, while she sang to him with her clear, ringing voice :

> "Life passes away,
>   To rich and to poor ;
> Delight will not stay,
>   Youth may not endure.
> Grandly or lowly,
>   In pleasure or pain,
> Quickly or slowly,
>   It comes not again.
>
> " A bird at sunrise
>   Re-sounds its sweet tune ;
> Into empty skies
>   Sails swiftly a moon.
> Earth, parch'd and lonely,
>   Is freshen'd by rain ;
> It is Life only
>   Returns not again."

As Freda sang the last word, Benjamin cried out delighted, " Again, again !" But

37—2

some little sound that Mr. Percival made un-intentionally, startled her, and looking round she beheld him.

She rose from her knees, blushing.

" This is Benjamin," she said simply.

" Don't let him take you away from me, dear," said the sick boy.

" No, never! no one shall do that, Benny."

She smiled gaily at him, and blew him a kiss from the tips of her pretty fingers as she spoke.

He laughed and clapped his hands feebly. Poor little hands! they were thinner and more skinny than when we saw them last. His face, too, was of a more ghastly white colour, and his eyes shone more brightly, and seemed more preternaturally large.

He fixed them eagerly on Mr. Percival's face, till that gentleman dropped his beneath the gaze, and then he said suddenly :

" And do you love her very much indeed, too ?"

Freda's blushes rose again at the question, but she stopped his mouth with her rosy kissing lips.

" Oh, hush ! Benny," she cried. " Every-

body does not love me like you, you know.
You and I are fast friends, and so we love
each other."

"Yes, and he loves you also," said Benny,
quite contented. "Just you look in his face,
and you'll see he does."

Involuntarily Freda turned her eyes towards Mr. Percival's face as desired, but she
dropped them again the next moment; nor
had that face made the same revelations to
her, that it had to Benny.

"I turned in to shelter from the heavy
rain, Mrs. Fane," he said quietly. "I had
not the least idea you were here. I did not
know," he added, smiling, "that this was
Benjamin's home, or that I should find you
singing here."

"Sing again," said the sick child imperatively.

And without one look at Mr. Percival, apparently without one thought for him, Freda
instantly obeyed.

> "Sweetest of surprises,
>   Unexpected thought,
> When the moon uprises,
>   Sudden and unsought,

> Floating like a silver tune
>   O'er the happy sea,
> Oh ! thou lovely little moon,
>   Dear thou art to me !
>
> " Very fair and stately,
>   Through the sky she goes,
> Like a queen who lately
>   Hath o'ercome her foes ;
> Glittering through trees of June,
>   Brightness to impart,
> Oh ! thou lovely little moon,
>   Shine into my heart !"

Benjamin listened with breathless delight, and laughed and clapped his poor hands when she ceased.

Mr. Percival listened also.   He had placed one hand before his eyes, so that his face was partly concealed.

" Do you not like it ? Does it make you cry ?" asked little Benjamin.

Freda turned, and seemed for the first time to remember his existence.

He removed his hand from his face.

" No, I am not crying," he said ; and he smiled ; but it was a wan, painful smile.

" Didn't you hear her sing before ?" persisted Benny.

"No, he never heard me before, my pet," she replied for him, gaily. "He is only a man, you know. I keep my songs for you."

"*Did* I never hear you before?" he said, in such an odd manner that she looked at him again.

"Surely not," she answered doubtfully. "We have not been musical, have we? And I hate singing properly to a piano. I sing in snatches just when they come."

"Yet you are very much——" He stopped himself suddenly, and coloured scarlet; then added, in a slow, rather artificial manner, "You have taken lessons, I am sure."

"There was a singing man in Jamaica who taught me, whether I would or no, and I think he improved me. But you are a critic, I suppose, Mr. Percival, knowing at once by a voice's sound whether it has been instructed or not. I never think of those things in singing. I just *hear*, and if I am pleased I care for nothing else."

"Yes, of course," he replied quietly. "Pleasure is the only thing to think about in anything."

"I like being pleased," replied Freda simply, "and I like giving pleasure."

"Indeed you do," said Benny's mother, who had just entered the room from one within it, and stood on the other side of his bed. "Of all the kind, good, benevolent, self-sacrificing young creatures I ever did see, you're the most. Whatever my poor boy would have done without you, or whatever he will do when you go—there, there, Benjamin, don't be silly; the lady's not going yet."

For Benny's poor little face had all shrivelled up, with the effort to keep back the tears that forced themselves out of his eyes, at the idea only of Freda's possible departure.

Then Freda was on her knees again by his side, kissing that sad young face.

"Don't, Benny! don't!" she cried. "I'll not go, never, as long as you want me. I'll never desert my Benny—never!"

"I'll be dead soon," said he, rubbing his cheek against hers, and then kissing her fervently.

"As long as you are alive, I'll stay here; I will indeed, Benny. I *promise*. Don't cry! don't be unhappy! Oh! please be happy, Benny!"

Mr. Percival looked on in mute amazement. Perhaps he was reflecting, was this the girl he had not an hour ago called heartless? Perhaps he was judging himself for uncharitable judgment. Nothing was more evident than that Freda was thinking only of Benny, and not wasting a thought as to what effect her words might produce on anybody else. Nothing was clearer than that she meant her promise with her whole heart. It was all as genuine and sincere as possible. But would she keep it if tried? And if she did not, could she be blamed for not doing so? Could any young, rich, beautiful lady be expected to make her plans depend on the wishes and wants of a poor, bedridden little boy. At all events, one thing was evident; Freda was not heartless, nor was she consciously living to please herself alone. She *did* wish to give pleasure to others, and that not only when the so doing was in any way reflected back on herself.

Freda disengaged herself gently from the boy's kisses.

"Now it is fine, and I must run away home," she cried brightly. "Corabel will be wondering and thinking I am lost. Whatever did bring you here, Mr. Percival?" she added as the two left the cottage together.

"I had been calling at your house—set off for a walk in the country, and took shelter from the rain."

"How oddly things always do come about," said Freda with the air of a philosopher; "you might have been a stranger, and I might have been somebody else."

"Might we really?" said Mr. Percival; "but why might not *I* have been the somebody else?"

"Only because you are not," she answered promptly. "Once I used to think it would be fun if the world was a masquerade, and none of us what we seemed. I wished all to be play—but I don't now—I am *content*, more content than I ever felt before. I am *glad* we are ourselves."

"And you are quite sure that we *are* ourselves, then?"

"Yes," she cried, laughing, "I am quite

quite sure; I would not be anything but myself now on any account."

"And that of course settles the question,"
he said quietly.

"Mr. Percival!" she cried, with sudden
impulse, "do you like Corabel *very* much?"

"Of course I do; no one can help liking
her."

"What did you and she talk about just
now?"

He looked hard at her.

"We talked about *you*."

She laughed.

"What could you two, always with me,
find to say about me? As long as you have
me, why should you talk about me? It is
the far-off we have need to talk about."

"We spoke of the far-off," he answered her
gravely. "Of what, I think, must seem to
you very far off indeed—of your marriage—
of—your husband."

He kept his eyes fixed on her, as he slowly,
almost reluctantly, uttered the last three
words; and she shrank, as she heard them,
like one on whom sharp physical pain has
been inflicted.

"Oh, don't," she cried. She put up her hands, as if almost to defend herself, and shivered.

"It is so dreadful for you even to think of it," he said, and you might have thought he was suffering with her. "You must have been very unhappy."

"I was *miserable!*" she cried; "it was horrible—I cannot *bear* to think of it."

"Child, was he unkind to you?—did he *beat* you?"

"I would not have cared if he had," she said, with a sort of recklessness; "it was worse—much worse—he did not love me."

"He did not love you! Are you *sure* he did not love you?"

"How could he? He *thought* he did—but he didn't. He loved some one else and believed it was me, and when he found me he couldn't bear me."

"And did you love him?"

"I!" she cried, "oh, I hated him."

"And do not you think perhaps he was to be pitied, if he *did* love you, and discovered you had never loved him?"

"Don't say so; I do hope he wasn't.

Sometimes the idea flashes across me, but it is so horrid I could not keep it. A man— a very good man—said to me, ' Child, have you no heart ? You have broken his heart— you have wrecked his life.' But it couldn't be—it couldn't—couldn't be. Then I should have to repent ; and there is remorse, you know, and that would be too shocking. I am sure I should not be myself then;" and as she spoke she grew pale as if in fear.

" If you ever love any one," said he, " you will then learn to pity him."

" Oh, I hope I shan't," she cried eagerly. " I used to pity myself so very *very* much, it never occurred to me to pity him. I *can't* think he really was to be pitied. I ran away from him, and he said nothing would ever make him take me back, or allow me to come back. I was delighted. But surely you don't pity him after that ?"

" But you ran away from him."

" Yes, of course I ran away from him."

" If he *did* love you—perhaps passionately (do you know what *that* means ?) — if he found you had never loved him, if you ran away from him, and if he said he would not take you back—I pity him more than any other living man I ever heard of."

Freda stared in his face, their eyes met, and something in his sent a thrill all through her—like terror—like despair. She could not tell what it meant, or why she felt as she did; but she suddenly stopped short, wrung her hands wildly, and bursting into tears rushed from his side, into her own house which they had just reached.

CHAPTER XII.

VISITORS.

MR. UNDERWOOD and Maud were breakfasting together with feelings as serene as the summer morning outside, when the gently-exciting daily occurrence of letters took place. Maud always got a letter every day—one letter—and always directed in the same hand—she, whose correspondence had been so small that often for weeks together the postman need not have called at any house where she dwelt alone. These letters, as familiar and as necessary as her breakfast, had ceased even to bring a blush into her fair pure cheek, though her eyes did shine with a soft lustre as she took them from her brother's willing hand. The Vicar generally received two or three postal communications every morning, but seldom any of special or thrilling interest. On this summer day, however, as he smilingly said " Here it is," and gave Maud her daily bread, his eyes fell on a square envelope directed to himself in a fine, dashing, yet feminine hand, which he well remembered, and which sent the colour into his face, though Maud's letter had not had that effect on hers.

He turned it over almost fearfully, and held it in his hand examining the outside of it, as people do examine the outsides of letters as if they would rather learn the story they are to tell from *that,* than from the worthless words that lie within. It is not on foreign paper, he thought wistfully ; and indeed it was not on foreign paper, for Freda affected the thickest kind that could be purchased ; and then he glanced furtively at Maud. But Maud was smiling over her own despatch, and was not thinking of him.

So, softly and timidly, and rather as if touching it might burn his fingers, the Vicar opened his letter. He glanced at the beginning and he glanced at the end, and then he read the missive attentively through from the first word to the last.

It ran thus :

"MY DEAR SIR,

"Very often have I thought of you and your sister, and I am sure you have neither of you forgotten me. You were so kind, and kind people don't forget. It was a good time, those sweet summer days, when I nursed her, and she dreamt that dream (how is Professor Stubbs ? bless him !), and I gathered peas in the garden. Do you remember wanting to send me to school ? Do you remember it all ? Ah, how nice it was ! yes, it *was* nice. Jamaica did not do— so here I am, and Corabel is with me. Will you come, you and Maud ? Do come and stay with us. I should like it, would not you ?

"Yours affectionately and gratefully,

"FREDA."

The Vicar read the note through three times before his colour had subsided, his smiles disappeared, and his face resumed its usual expression. Then he turned to address his sister, but she was still fully occupied with her own letter.

"Oh, Lewes," she said, with modest pride, "only think; Arthur has been called in to a duchess, he has indeed — the Duchess of Dashminster—and he has done her a great deal of good, and is becoming quite the fashion. How clever he is, and how successful!"

"Yes," answered the Vicar, his thoughts so occupied that his mind could not take in what she said, "that is always the way, isn't it?"

"What?" asked Maud, surprised : "but he is rather tiresome," and here she blushed mildly—"he is impatient ; I can't think why men are impatient. He *will* talk about the autumn, Lewes."

"About the autumn?" questioned Lewes, with vague stupidity ; "what harm is there in talking about the autumn?"

Maud turned her meek reproachful eyes on the Vicar.

"Oh, Lewes," she cried, "do you wish to get rid of me?"

" My dearest Maud !" he exclaimed, recalled
to the present moment, and to what was being
said to him, more by her manner than even by
her words, " how can you say such a thing ?
Only just think what a lonely fellow I shall
be without you; and then suppose for a
moment that I can be in any hurry for your
marriage. No, my dear, I must bear it when
it comes, and bear it cheerfully for your sake,
because I am sure it will make you an uncommonly happy woman. But as for myself——"

" Yes, it is a great pity," said Maud
regretfully, " that Arthur cannot live in the
country, or you in London. Separations are
sad things, and if *you* could ever marry,
Lewes——"

" To be sure," said Mr. Underwood, laughing, " if I could ever, or if ever I could marry,
it would simplify matters very much; but I
am afraid I have the cut of an old bachelor
about me, and we need not think of *that*. So
now tell me, my dear, what is it this Arthur
of yours says about the autumn?"

Maud again blushed mildly.

" This Arthur of mine," she said, repeating

the expression as if it gave her pleasure, "speaks of the autumn as the time when London doctors take their holidays, and seems to think there is only one use can be made of the holiday. What can I say to him, Lewes ?"

She looked rather anxiously at him, as if she wished for advice, but would be sorry if the advice was not of one particular kind.

"Well, really, my dear Maud," he said, "I don't see what there is to wait for. It has been a long acquaintance, and not a short engagement, and I think our friend's wishes are reasonable as well as natural."

Maud cast down her eyes and was silent, but I believe her brother's advice was what she wished it to be.

"I never can understand his having cared for me all these years," she said, "and no one having the least idea of it."

"We were blind," said Lewes, "and our minds full of other notions."

"Such a man as Arthur to have cared for me when we were both so young, and to have gone on caring for me ever since, though we never met and he never heard of me—it is indeed incomprehensible; and then that we should meet after all. Lewes, marriages *are* made in heaven."

" Yes, happy marriages are, Maud."

" He fancied poor Mr. Fane cared for me," said Maud, uttering the name of her early love calmly, but with feeling, " and would never have spoken if he had not known he was married. From that moment he determined to find me if he could. Fancy, when I was so sickly and growing old—I am not far from thirty, you know, Lewes—his still being quite unchanged."

"Talking of poor Fane," said the Vicar, "I had a letter from Freda this morning."

" From Freda! a letter from Freda! Oh, Lewes, why did not you tell me?"

" I am telling you, and you were so busy with your own letter, you could not attend to me before."

" How is she, Lewes? is she still in Jamaica? what does she say?"

" She has come home; she is at S——, in Dorsetshire, and she wants us to go and stay with her."

" Not really? What a pleasant idea! Could

we not do it, Lewes ? Would not you like it ?"

"Yes, I should like it, and I don't see why we shouldn't do it. It is not a very long journey, and the change would be good for you."

After this conversation it is hardly necessary to say that Dr. Hilton's visit to the Vicarage had been made. He there devoted himself to Maud, paying her quiet, constant, and unobtrusive attention. At the end of a few weeks he offered, and was accepted, and then he told Maud the, to her, wonderful story, of how he had loved her ever since he had first known her, and of why he had not felt hopeless of success, and it was only when she had become accustomed to the tranquil happiness of a second love, that she was informed of the death of the man who had unintentionally gained her girlish affections. Under the circumstances she bore the sad intelligence very well, though her grief was sincere, and the knowledge of his death recalled the past, with all its joys and its sorrows, its hope and its despair.

The Vicar was exceedingly pleased at his

sister's engagement, as he was too good and unselfish a man to grieve on his own account, for that which he felt would secure to her an unusual amount of earthly happiness. He, too, was surprised ; but still there *was* nothing more natural than that Maud should be loved and appreciated. He did not know the man to whom he would so gladly have given his sister as Arthur Hilton ; and Maud's delicate health, her weak nerves, and easily-depressed spirits, made it a very desirable thing that her husband should be well off, and a member of the medical profession. Maud required a great deal of care, of looking after, and o constant cheerful kindness, and all this she would get in the pleasantest and most sensible manner, from him, who had chosen her for his wife. The Vicar's heart might sink a little as he thought of his own lonely future, but he was not a man to give way ; and he felt certain that all was and must be for the best, and that he was strong enough for whatever might be before him.

And so the brother and sister accepted Freda's invitation and arranged to go to S—— for the present, while the autumn was fixed as the time for Maud's marriage, and her quiet preparations were already begun for that important event. Freda did not tell Corabel that she had invited the Underwoods, or that they had agreed to come. She thought it would be extremely amusing to say nothing about it, and to let these people, of whom she had talked so much to her, walk quietly into the drawing-room as if it belonged to them, before Corabel had heard a word of their being expected. She was delighted to get their rooms prepared in secret without her friend knowing anything about it; and she went laughing through the house, charmed at the idea of all she was doing and concealing, and at the surprise she was preparing for Corabel.

"And then the nicest thing that could happen would be for Mr. Underwood to marry Corabel; for if he did, he could not want to marry *me*, and his wanting to marry me would be the only drawback to it all."

So thought Freda as she put the finishing-touches to Maud's room on the day when she expected her arrival.

She determined to persuade Corabel to go

out before the hour came, and so to receive them alone; and make Maud take off her things and be seated in the drawing-room, and Lewes too, and then for Corabel to come back and be *so* astonished. "And I will make her guess who they are, and not tell her unless she guesses right; no, not if it is for the whole time of their visit," cried Freda, and laughed aloud, enraptured at this last brightest of bright ideas.

Freda looked rather anxiously at herself in the glass that day.

"I wonder whether I am quite as pretty now as I was then?" she thought, with a touch of anxiety. "I should not like to be gone off; and somehow I think I am a little. I hope not; Corabel would tell me;" then aloud, "Corabel, do you think I am gone off at all?"

"Gone off, Freda! what can you mean?"

"Oh, don't you know what going off means? Very well then, am I as pretty as I was? I am growing older every day—do I show it? am I changed?"

At that Corabel laughed. "You *are* a little changed," she began.

"Oh, Corabel, am I really?"

"Yes, but indeed, Freda, it is only for the better; your figure is more formed, and you have more expression in your face—a great deal more—but you are quite as pretty as ever; nay, you are prettier; I think you grow prettier every day."

"Do you?" cried she, blushing, smiling, and very much pleased. "Corabel, I *am* glad."

"And I think I know somebody who agrees with me," said Corabel, a little slyly.

"No you don't; nobody can, for they none of them knew me long ago; and you did, so you are the only person who can really judge, and that is why I thought I would ask you. Corabel, I wonder what makes you so very good? I am getting puzzled about people being good and bad by nature."

"Is my not considering you gone off the proof of my goodness?"

"Not at all! Such an idea! I had flown away miles from that. I was thinking of something quite different, and that brought me to one of my puzzles. If you were all alike it would not matter; but you are *not* alike, and that is what puzzles me."

" What are you talking about, Freda?"

." Of you and Maud Underwood, of course; what else should I be talking about? You are both of you good by nature, and you are both of you quiet; you are neither of you lively or care for things, and yet you are as different from each other as you are from—— me! *You* are strong, and calm, and firm, and know what you're about; she is weak, and yielding, and nervous—a wee bit fussy (*nice* fussiness, you know, she is all nice)— and has to be managed for."

" But why *should* we be alike, Freda?"

" Oh, I don't know. Can't you see? If you can't, I'm sure I can't explain it. Nobody ever can explain anything—unless one knows by instinct, one never knows. Nobody ever yet made any of my puzzles the least bit clearer to me. Oh, Corabel, I wish you would go out."

At that Corabel began to laugh.

" Thanks for your politeness, dear; but why should I go out?"

" I want these wools matched, and I want

these books changed, and I don't want to go out myself."

" Is Mr. Percival coming to call, I wonder?" thought Corabel.

She thought it, but she did not say it. Freda never sent her on errands ; she would far rather run on one herself than send Corabel, towards whom her conduct was regulated by the perfection of delicacy and affection, not ceremonious, and so reminding her of the real difference in their positions, yet not treating her in any way as the " companion " or " humble friend.".

Corabel felt that there must be some reason why Freda wished her to match the wools and change the books to-day, so she gladly and quickly complied with her wishes.

As soon as the shades of green, blue, and yellow had been taken, and the resemblances and differences of what were required clearly understood, and the novels placed in Corabel's hand, with the strict injunction not to get anything " stupid " in exchange ; as soon as the house-door had closed on her friend, and Freda had watched her retreating figure till it turned the corner of the terrace and was lost to sight, she gave a little cry of delight and waltzed round the room, clapping her pretty rosy palms together.

" What a manager I am," she cried, " what a strategist! I ought to be Talleyrand *and* Bismark ; I know I ought. What a mistake it is that I am only Freda! Europe has had a loss, though S—— may have gained by it." And then she laughed gleefully. " Now I should like to dress up as a servant. Oh, why did I leave that *dear* dress at Roseberry Farm ? Letty did not appreciate it, and looked mildly miserable when I wore it, and now it would be worth its weight in gold to me. Shall I ask Ann ? Shall I borrow her clothes ? Alas ! it would be useless. Ann's costume in nothing marks her as a servant— it is just a poor imitation of mine."

While she was still laughing, dancing, and soliloquising, a cab drove up to the door with luggage on the roof, and a gentleman jumped out of it, and then turned to assist a lady to descend. Freda was actually startled at the arrival of her expected guests at just the very time when, according to " Bradshaw," they ought to arrive. She stood suddenly still, then stepped on tip-toe to the window. There she saw Maud, her hand on the Vicar's shoulder, stepping from the cab to the pavement.

" How well she looks ; what a *sweet* look she has got in her face ! Oh, the dear ! how nice it is to see her ! And he is quite unchanged, the dear, good man ! I *do* like you, Mr. Underwood. If you want me to marry you, I don't see why I shouldn't. You *have* got the nicest face. It is all better even than I expected. I could jump over the moon for joy."

And so Freda ran nimbly from the room to the staircase, and there into Maud's arms, from which kind receptacle she held out both hands to clasp those of the Vicar ; and then, to her own great surprise, and the surprised pleasure also of her friends, she found she was crying.

She hastily and eagerly called out to them that she was as glad as ever she could be, and had not the least idea why the tears came.

" I never understood Miranda before," she said, smiling through the unexpected tears ;

"but I am a fool to cry at what I am so exceedingly glad of."

And so she kissed Maud again, and again shook hands with Lewes.

When they were in the drawing-room, she took off Maud's jacket and hat, and put her into an easy-chair and brought her a foot-stool : and then she made the Vicar a bob-curtsey and gave him a sly look, and said, in her vulgar accent, " Lor', don't you know that I'm the new servant ?"

And then she laughed her silvery lady-laugh, and said :

" Oh, you dear people! oh, you good people! how nice, how *extra* nice it is !"

With such a great emphasis on the extra, that she had to draw a deep breath afterwards to rest herself.

The Vicar and Maud were charmed at the effusion of her joy, and felt its sweet fascina-tion in the very depths of their hearts, and if they were quieter and calmer than she was —as it was their natures to be—they were hardly less glad.

" Why you have grown taller," said Maud.

" No. Have I really ?" laughed Freda.

" That is a very young thing to do. But as for you, Miss Underwood, you look *quite* different. You have *such* a different look— hasn't she ?" to the Vicar.

" She is in better health, and shows it in her face," replied he.

" Is that all ?" asked Freda, with a feeling akin to disappointment. " Will health do *that ?* She used to have a wistful look in her eyes, and now they shine with content. Is it only health ?"

" Why, Freda, you are a witch," replied Maud Underwood, and she blushed as well as laughed.

Freda looked at her curiously. Something new and strangely sweet had lately stolen into her own life, unrecognised by her, un- conscious to herself, which made her quick with thoughts and perceptions, on one subject, at least.

" Is it possible ?" she said softly. " Are you—? do you— ?" she paused to look her questions.

" She will tell you all about it," cried the Vicar ; " and some day, I hope, we shall introduce him to you."

"Tell me instantly," cried she imperiously, "this moment, who is he? and when?"

"He is Dr. Hilton," replied the obedient Vicar, yielding of course to Freda's despotism, as everybody who came near her did; "a very old friend, and the time is to be the autumn."

"Dr. Hilton! Why I have seen him; I have heard of him. He looks rather so-so; but is clever, very clever, and is to be one of the first doctors in Europe. He was a friend of——"

Here she paused, and glanced appealingly from one to the other, as if to ask them how they *could?* Exactly as if it had been they, not she, who had so nearly uttered the forbidden name.

But Maud's face was grave, and she said :

"What can you mean, by looking rather ' so-so ' ?"

"Oh, you know what I mean—you must know. He is a little smallish, and one does not think about him. But that does not really matter. *Is* he taller than you are, Maud ?" she added, abruptly and anxiously.

"Oh dear, yes ; several inches. You really

have made a great mistake, Freda. He is not a very short man. He is quite the middle height. The idea of his not being taller than I am !"

"That's all right," said Freda approvingly. "Then the rest does not signify one bit."

Maud still did not look satisfied. She had not Corabel's quiet sense of humour, which made her get on so very comfortably with the wild girl, and she now felt a little uneasy in her mind ; and, as a matter of course, looked to Lewes to help her, which, as a matter of course, he did.

"Hilton is nice-looking, a thorough gentleman, and his face improves *very* much on acquaintance. He has a twinkle in his eye and a fund of dry humour which will amuse you greatly, Mrs. Fane."

"Has he ? I am so glad. Then he'll do," said Freda calmly. "And now have some tea, my dear people—let me give you tea." And she eagerly poured it out for them ; but, as she presented Lewes with his cup, she said beseechingly : "*Don't* call me Mrs. Fane."

He coloured and smiled, while he took the cup from her hand, and looked down into the transparent depths of her eyes—eyes not less transparent than when he had last looked into them, but, as it now suddenly struck him, with deeper depths. What had she been doing since they parted at Roseberry Farm? Had she felt? Had she suffered?

Just then, while Freda faced him with eager grace (her back to the door), holding out the cup of tea, which he slowly took from her hand, gazing with startled eagerness down into her wonderful eyes as he did so, a light step was heard outside, the door opened, and Corabel strolled carelessly in.

"I have done all you wanted, dear," she began saying, when she became aware that there were visitors in the room. Visitors? The lady had her head uncovered, the gentleman was taking his tea like an inhabitant of the house, and looking into the face of its mistress meantime, like—what? The gentleman—was she dreaming? Was she mad? *Who* was he? Who *could* he be, as he *could* not be what he was? And he looked at her too, attracted not only by her entrance, but by the sudden, abrupt pause in her steps and words, and perhaps, also, by the sound of her voice.

The man and the woman stared at each other in a dazed, amazed manner; for her effect on Lewes was quite as great as Lewes's on her, and then they both at the same moment spoke, and each uttered a name in astonished, incredulous tones.

" Lewes !" cried she.

" Anna !" ejaculated he.

" Are you both mad ?" exclaimed Freda ; and, if she had not grasped the cup which she thought he had taken hold of, it would have fallen on the ground between her and the Vicar.

" Is it really you ?" he said eagerly, not in the least attending to Freda.

Corabel advanced a step or two, and held out her hand. She looked very white. There was no colour in her face, not even in her lips ; but she was perfectly calm and composed.

" It is a great surprise," she said.

" Good heavens !" cried the Vicar. " Are you Corabel ?"

Her white face became crimson. She gave a sad little smile.

"Yes," she said, " I am Corabel."

"What *does* it all mean?" cried Freda. "Why does he call you Anna? Why does he ask if you are Corabel? Are you an impostor? Do you go by two names?"

"I *have* two names," replied her friend, quite calm now. "Anna Cora, but I was always called Anna when—Mr. Underwood knew me." There was a pause before she said "Mr. Underwood." "No one ever called me Cora but you."

"To be sure," cried Freda. "I had quite forgotten. You were Miss Bell to everybody else, and I found your name in one of your books, 'Anna Cora Bell.' So it was, of course; and I said I would call you Corabel, and I quite forgot about the Anna."

Here Miss Underwood, who had left her easy-chair and footstool, and stood in rather a nervous manner, glancing from her brother to Corabel, and from Corabel to her brother, trembling a little, and getting first pale and then pink, and then pale again, spoke :

"Do you remember me, too, Miss Bell?" she said. "I am Maud Underwood."

"I remember you very well, indeed," said Corabel; and the two ladies shook hands, but without *empressement*, almost without cordiality.

"I hope," said Lewes, "that you have been quite well and happy, Miss Bell, since we—since I last saw you."

"Thanks, I am quite well," she replied. That seemed to be all she was going to say; but, with a great effort, she spoke again: "My poor father died two years ago."

"Ah!" he answered. "I am very sorry for you."

"I think, Freda, I will go and take my things off; and is it not almost time to dress for dinner?"

"Yes; quite, I think. Let us all go to our rooms. But how curious it is you two—you three, I mean—should have known each other, and I not know it. Corabel," sud-

denly, " why did you never tell me you knew
my Vicar ?"

Corabel's whole face in one instant became
scarlet. The depth of the blush looked absolutely painful on so pale a face. She felt
herself touched there, and knew not what to
say.

" I—could not be sure—it was the same,"
she faltered.

" Then why didn't you say something, and
make sure ?" answered Freda sharply. " And
Underwood is not such a common name ; nor
is Lewes or Maud."

Corabel was perfectly silent, but the Vicar
came quietly to her assistance.

" We knew Miss Bell during her father's
lifetime, and it may be distressing to her now
to recall old times."

" Poor Corabel !" cried Freda, instantly
appeased ; and Corabel, with some emotion,
left the room.

" That is it, I suppose," said Freda, looking
appealingly at Lewes. " She never speaks
of the past. I did not know she ever had a
father."

" Yes, she had once, and he was a rich man.

It is a great surprise to find her circumstances so different. Mr. Crawford spoke of her as your—companion."

"Mr. Crawford is an idiot and a wretch! She is my very dear and very kind friend. We *love* each other."

END OF VOL. II.

BILLING AND SONS, PRINTERS, GUILDFORD, SURREY.

R. T. T.